MW01283352

A Catskill Journey

By Paul H. Zimmerman

Library of Congress Cataloguing-in-Publication Data

A Catskill Journey
/ Paul H. Zimmerman

ISBN	KINDLE	978-1-950392-84-1
ISBN	PAPERBACK	978-1-950392-83-4
ISBN	HARDBACK	978-1-950392-82-7
ISBN	AUDIO	978-1-950392-85-8

This story is a work of historical fiction. However, the author endeavored to make this book an accurate representation of the time and locations.

Ahead of The Press Publishing
St. Louis, Missouri

Table of Contents

Acknowledgements

To my wonderful parents, for giving me a good mind and always encouraging me to use it.

To my late Uncle Gilbert, who taught me the value of knowledge.

To Liesha Crawford, for her insightful, detailed, and invaluable book editing.

To Captain, to whom I am very grateful for her support, encouragement, and excellent editing of this book.

And to my family, whose love and support allowed me to write this book.

Dedication

This book is dedicated to all whose passion is to keep people and places alive through their writing.

A Catskill Journey

By Paul H. Zimmerman

A Catskill Journey Map

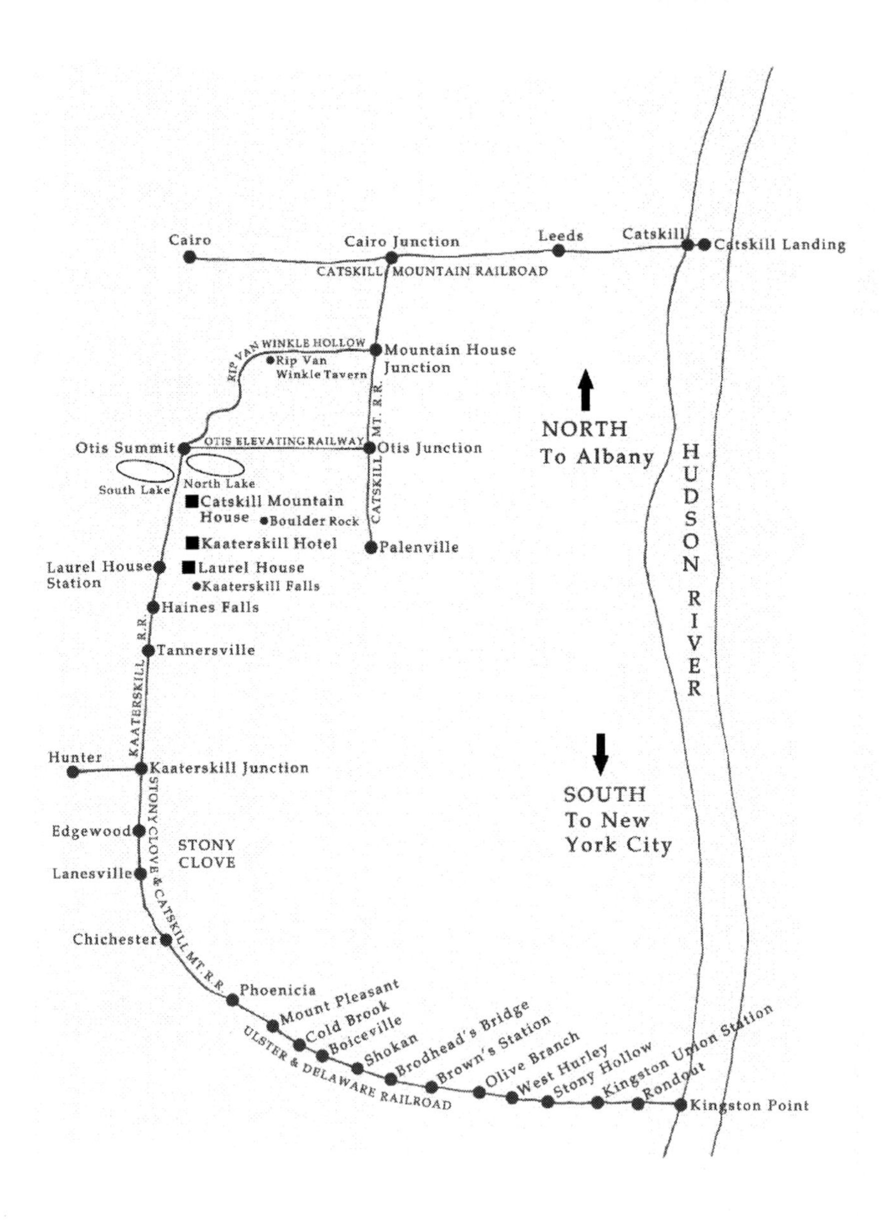

The Hudson River Day Line

The Steamship *Albany* of the Hudson River Day Line

I'm back in New York now. It is late August in the city, and the leaves are already beginning to hint of autumn to come. Memory of my Mountain House visit a month ago is both pleasurable and painful, for I love her, but had to return to my work in the city. My friend and business associate Andrew was correct, I would never forget the beauty of the Catskills.

I remember when he first told me about the Mountain House, having experienced a few days of clean skies, great views and fine hospitality in the previous summer of 1891. Andrew's descriptions for the days after he returned were repetitious but intriguing.

The cost factor was at first prohibitive, but I convinced myself it would be worthwhile. After all, I deserved a good vacation. Living in New York City can take a toll on one's spirit and I felt the need to be refreshed. The life of an accountant can be toilsome and darn right boring. When I finally made the decision to visit the Mountain House, I was pleased with myself, for I was determined to relax and enjoy the "Finest view in the world".

I left my apartment on Sunday morning July 3rd, 1892. The excitement of my journey had kept me awake most of the night. I awoke with the birds and set about getting my things in order. As I took the carriage to the dock, I was surprised by the activity so early in the morning. Street vendors were already preparing their wares on the sidewalks; policemen, fishermen and others were going about their work.

I had that uneasy feeling that so often occurs when one is on vacation, one of guilt that you can enjoy yourself in the presence of so many who must work while you relax. That feeling also meant that I was beginning my well-deserved vacation, and I reveled in the fact that such guilty emotions would soon vacate.

The weather was fine, with the hint of summer humidity and sunshine. Arriving at the dock I was pleasantly surprised by the ship that would take me to my destination. I purchased my ticket, checked my luggage, and walked over the gangplank onto the ship. As I stepped aboard the steamship *Albany*, one of the "Hudson River Day Line Steamers" advertised on pamphlets and banners all over the city, I was personally assured by a crew member the journey would be both "Comfortable and entertaining." I wondered if he would espouse the same amenities on a cloudy cold morning.

Anyway, I was too excited to waste my time below deck. Deciding to test the hospitality of the crew I quickly secured a prime spot on the forward starboard deck so I could ask questions about the sights we were to pass.

There was a slight jerk of the boat as we pulled away from the dock, and we were on our way. The steam engines spurted for a moment and soon reached their maximum power, spewing a warm mist from the tall, black pipes on all those who chose to view the New York skyline with me on the top deck. It is an impressive city, and if you ever doubted such a claim, there was always someone nearby to reassure you of such a fact. There is nothing wrong with being proud of the place you live, but the typical New Yorker can carry that belief a little beyond sensibility.

The air already seemed to be clearing, and I convinced myself that it was all in my imagination for we were hardly out of sight of the city. The morning mist was burning off the Hudson River. Birds were flying overhead, and I chastised myself for being unable to identify a single variety. Growing up in New York can be both enlightening and restrictive. I know where every museum, drinking fountain, public restroom and carriage stop exist in the largest city in the world.

But I was seriously deficient in the knowledge of the natural world around me. Birds had always been an annoyance, and suddenly appreciating their beauty in the open air above the water glistening in the morning sunlight had renewed my interest in learning more.

The steamship *Albany* was a large vessel capable of fifteen hundred passengers on its three decks. A narrow but long ship, with large flags at the stern and bow that flapped noisily as we moved swiftly up the Hudson.

Andrew had mentioned that I would pass some truly beautiful sights on my journey to the Mountain House, and I was anxious to experience them all. The immensity of this grand river can be deceiving from the shore. I had been fortunate to have friends invite me for the occasional sailing excursion on the Hudson and enjoyed those times.

The steamship *Albany* of the Hudson River Day Line
near the Hudson River Palisades

This was different. The Hudson is miles wide where it empties into the Atlantic in New York harbor. Waves were breaking against the side of our steamship, and I noticed myself feeling slightly queasy.

My self-pity was interrupted by the gruff voice of a sailor who obviously earned his living with the muscles in his back. For a moment I didn't understand what he was saying, I only noticed the calluses on his hands and the sunburned crags of his weatherworn face. The life of an accountant may be boring, but I certainly have never known the strains of a job the likes of which this man endured daily working this ship.

I decided to suppress my guilt of an easier life long enough to hear him say that I might get a better view portside. Moving as directed, I was pleasantly surprised by the beauty of the Hudson River Palisades - cliffs that rise out of the Hudson with an occasional beautiful house perched on the crest. I envied their views of the river. Between the changes in seasons and Hudson River activity, it must be captivating.

The dual "whoosh!" sound of the ship drew my interest, and I was fascinated by the steam engine powering our way through the water. This ship was typical of the steamships I had observed previously on the Hudson, consisting of large paddlewheels centered on both sides of the ship.

The first "whoosh!" sound is the engine driving the paddlewheels with a large, forged iron arm attached on the side of the paddlewheels. The second "whoosh!" sound is the steam spewing out of the tall stacks centered on the ship. I worked my way to the top deck of the *Albany* where my view was much better.

As we continued slowly but surely up the Hudson River, I noticed an impressive Scottish-style castle on an island with the name "Bannerman's Island" visible on the structure. Obviously positioned to be viewed by the less fortunate without island castles who happened to pass by on the river, Bannerman made sure that his name etched in stone at the top of the castle faced the channel.

A tinge of jealousy rushed up my spine as I wondered about the splendor of viewing sunsets from the top of one's personal castle on the Hudson. My attention turned to the people aboard the many sailing ships of all sizes surrounding the *Albany,* using the beauty of the Hudson for their pleasure.

I found a comfortable bench on the top deck and sat for the first time on board. I realized my child-like excitement had prevented me from the lull of contentment, but I was resolved to pursue personal respite on this vacation. While pondering when the comfort of my surroundings and the idea of not having to deal with numbers in a stuffy office would allow me to relax, I was startled from my personal thoughts by a young woman and her beau who sat next to me and decided to converse.

"Friends in Albany?" she questioned. Nervously I looked at her strapping young man and back at the woman.

"No, I am on the way to the Mountain House near Catskill," I offered, and she seemed pleased with my response.

"We are going on our honeymoon to the Laurel House," she said, and I nodded approvingly although I have never been to any of the Catskill hotels.

Legendary in both their inaccessibility and intensity of personal comforts, these hotels were frequented by many of my clients. Through snippets of many conversations, I gleaned they are situated along a high ridge on the west bank of the Hudson River named the Great Wall of Manitou by the natives.

Amenities abounded in these hotels. Although varied in their sophistication, I had been assured that fresh meat, milk, fruit, vegetables, and more, were provided from local gardens and markets.

"Why did you decide on the Laurel House?" I asked half-heartedly, to which she readily responded,

"It was not too expensive, and daddy spent a lot on our wedding already."

I wondered what career she pursued, but I determined she was probably not the sharpest nail in the bucket. I looked away in a manner that (hopefully) indicated our conversation would end soon if not immediately. Not rude, but New Yorkers know how to end frivolous undesired palavering. I wished the young couple well as they walked away arm-in-arm.

My decision to look portside rewarded me with a fine view of West Point Military Academy. Obviously named for its position jutting out into the Hudson from the west bank, a long, very tall wall faced our ship. Mentioned on previous visits to West Point by carriage, my memory was renewed about a large chain that was once installed across the river here at this former fort to prevent enemy ships from navigating the channel.

Knowing that many of the generals who commanded my father during the Civil War trained at West Point Academy gave me mixed feelings. As proud as I could have been of him, fate dictated that my father was wounded due to poor battle direction by young, inexperienced officers rushed into service directly from the academy.

Everyone originally, vastly, and incorrectly assumed the war would be over quickly. But the raw reality of a long, destructive, extremely deadly, and country-splitting war sadly set in to all involved. Our entire family had bitterly cursed the sad loss of the man we knew as our father, but was not that man who returned from battle. But I refused to dwell on such misfortune.

As we continued to move swiftly north up the majestic Hudson, I noticed the river was beginning to narrow and not so slightly. We passed steamships heading south named *M Martin*, and *Chauncey Vibbard*. Other large steamships passed us named *Mary Powell* and *New York*, proudly flying the Day Line's red and white flag as did our steamship *Albany*.

The ships gave a "toot!" and the captains waved to each other as we passed closely in the narrowing river channel. The Hudson was shared by small pleasure boats and large ships which all used the busy route for transportation. I wondered if the river bottom was also closer, and if the hull of this ship would ever come close to being bogged down in a low-level section of the river. Obviously, my experience in such matters as to the "river worthiness" of any vessel or especially a steamship such as the *Albany* was non-existent.

I comforted myself that many on the ship greeted me with smiles and I did not see the smallest amount of concern amongst them. Also, I knew that I could swim. My worries were abated at least for the moment, and I was forced to smile about my unjustified and urbane rumblings on a very safe ship.

The steep cliffs and jutting points of land we experienced before were replaced with round rolling hills of yellow, green, and brown blanketing the banks of the Hudson. How much work and drudgery must be extolled to not only completely change the landscape from forests to farmland but to then plow, plant and harvest the bountiful yield of that land? As an accountant, I might be able to help a farmer turn a profit from his harvest, but I would have no understanding of how to work the land.

The more I removed myself from the city, the more I admired the contributions the so-called "common man" donated to society.

Even from our distance in the river valley, the mountains were impressive in their height and sheer size. I was awed by the expansive splendor of it all and had to admire the fact that this is truly a country of beauty to be admired.

I was lulled by the consistent "whoosh!" sound of the steam engine and the paddlewheels. As I moved about the ship and continued to engage in small talk, I felt more comfortable with the ship, the water, and the land around us. Adding together fresh air and some sunshine, a beautiful boat ride, chatting with unfamiliar people and the anticipation of my first vacation at the Mountain House had placed me in a jolly good mood. A short and efficient stop at Poughkeepsie to exchange a few passengers and we headed back north.

We passed under the steel structure of a train bridge which loomed over our ship, impressively spanning the Hudson. An engineering achievement, I had read about the trestle construction in New York City newspapers and now found a deeper appreciation of its intricate steel beams and sheer size. I reminded myself of the trepidation I experienced when I first set foot on the planks of the ship and my unfounded fears of being grounded in the middle of the Hudson! I found myself feeling a bit melancholy if the trip were to end soon.

We quickly crossed the Hudson as it widened, and we approached a lighthouse on the left. As I passed an elderly couple, I heard the old gentleman say it was the "Rondout Lighthouse" near Kingston. Soon, activity on the shore near the lighthouse caught my eye and my curiosity.

I strained to take a closer look at the bustling business on the west bank while we passed the lighthouse, not affording me the best view. I could see why the lighthouse was there - to prevent ships from the dangerously low bottom near that west bank. Although the ship continued to steer clear, I was able to watch the stone works and shipping port in full operation.

Earlier thoughts of sympathy for the toil of the farm laborer were quickly replaced by the sheer magnitude of physical exertion moving those stones. Noted for their long-term wearability, and rough, non-slip surface even when wet, bluestone, as it is commonly called, is used extensively in New York City for sidewalks.

I had walked miles in the city on such bluestone, and infrequently witnessed stones delivered by oxen or horses and delicately positioned in place for a smooth walkway. The sheer magnitude of working the stone and moving it to New York had me yearning for a more intimate understanding of the business. As I leaned over the rail and continued to focus on the stone yard, I absorbed such an understanding.

We continued to stay clear of the lighthouse and my first observation from that distance were the piles of bluestone stacked neatly in several locations in the stone works yard. Men could be seen dragging carts with slabs of stone, and horses were used to drag carts with bigger stacks of stone to load on ships.

A huge active smokestack rose in the middle of numerous tan-colored one-to-three-storied buildings with gray rooftops set back from the vertical piles of stone. The similarity of the buildings gave the entire scene a resemblance to a child's toy village. Clouds of dust arose from a row of openings along a single-story section of one of the buildings. I assumed the particulate was caused by sawing, planing, and surface grinding the stone.

Several tall, green metal posts were cabled to the ground on the loading dock understandably for strength to counter the weight of the stone being transported at the end of swinging arms loading stone pallets onto waiting ships. As we passed, I counted no less than three ships preparing or being loaded with shipments meant for city sidewalks and buildings.

I observed nothing that resembled a quarry, which indicated the stone must have been transported to this location for shipment. The further we moved north away from the stone works location the less detail I was able to discern. Still, the magnitude of the work involved left me in awe.

I continued to walk around the decks of the ship, having exhausted my desire to start a conversation and was beginning to wish we would reach our destination soon. I reminded myself when we reached Catskill it would still be an arduous journey up the mountain road to the hotel. Andrew had offered that it would probably be better to take the new Otis Elevating Railway to the top.

The brochures distributed in the city pronounced the newly completed railway a "wonder of engineering" and a safe, marvelous rail ride up the Great Wall of Manitou. I decided it would be a more rustic, natural experience to take a carriage to the top instead.

I also had visions of a smelly, smoky ride in open-air rail cars up a steep dangerous incline behind a steam engine. As it was new, Andrew could neither agree nor disagree with my possible assessment. Consideration of either prospective mode of transportation did not improve my disposition at that moment. I just hoped it would be a quick and rewarding journey from the port of Catskill to the hotel.

The steamship *Albany* of the Hudson River Day Line
landing at Kingston Point

A large sign positioned between two roof peaks of a two-storied pavilion labeled "KINGSTON POINT PARK" was visible as our ship slowed and pulled up to the large dock at Kingston. Whereas the Poughkeepsie station was a few simple buildings, this was a beautiful park with a lagoon, walking trails with flowers and much more.

An Ulster and Delaware Railroad station was also visible near the dock. Since my departure travel plans included boarding a ship from Kingston Point, I was anxious to further explore the park when I returned in a few days.

As we left Kingston, where more passengers disembarked than boarded, I assumed due to the junction with the Ulster and Delaware Railroad, we rounded another lighthouse on a west point jutting out into the Hudson. It was a small, brick house with the lighthouse tower itself attached to the side of the building. As we passed the lighthouse the river narrowed, and the currents seemed to pick up slightly. The ship was now rocking more than before, and I felt the need to sit down.

Closing my eyes and setting my head against the wall I must have slept briefly as I was awakened by the ship's steward in his crisp, white outfit announcing a half-hour arrival in Catskill to the passengers as he passed from deck to deck. I hoped I hadn't been sleeping with my mouth agape and snoring on the bench. I noticed my earlier queasiness had subsided.

If I thought the river had narrowed earlier, I was mistaken, as the Hudson continued to surprise me how much narrower it is upstate than near New York City. Our surrounding land also continued to change and became more dotted with forests, and interspersed hedgerows of trees separating colored squares of different crops.

The Southernmost Catskill Mountains were beginning to reveal themselves through the distant mist. Although we passed brick kilns, ice warehouses, fishing and shipping ports, and other businesses along the river, my continued observation of the dwindling development along the shoreline and more dedication to rural pursuits led me to appreciate that this was true wilderness.

The romantic visions developed and extolled by modern writers about the wonders of the backwoods had often interested me. I loved reading tales of Indians and pioneers carving out an existence in the wild, learning to get along – or not. Intrigued by the prospect but apprehensive of the reality, I would not know how to survive in the woods for a day alone. Shivering against a tree, hoping someone would find me – those were my visions of such an experience.

Shaking such a nightmare out of my head, I noticed the ship began to slow and my anticipation rose as I assumed we must be getting close to our destination. My hunch was confirmed when one of the shipmates shouted, "Next stop - Catskill Landing", as he walked the deck with determination.

Maneuverability afforded by the independent side paddlewheels of the craft, we made another quick swing to the right and then left following the contours and narrows of the Hudson. During our journey we occasionally passed several small sailboats on the river. Now, however, the river was dotted with the white sails of many small sailing craft.

We passed an obviously uninhabited, heavily forested island to the right, and then to our left the outline and details of the city of Catskill came into view. The city is perched on a large, relatively flat area in a bend of the river, with a gradual slope leading up to the blueish Catskill Mountains in the distance.

Occasional peaks of church spires poked up from the surrounding lower, two-story buildings that lined the main street. As we swung into our dock, more detail became visible such as horse carriages and people walking. I perceived not the frantic, crowded pace of New York but a slower, more purposeful type of sensibility to even their walk.

As I wondered if I was reading too much into my initial perceptions, I noticed another large, three deck ship heading north toward Albany, I assumed. This ship was much larger than ours, and I wondered if it offered a steadier, less swaying experience to the patrons.

But I had more important things with which to ponder and concern myself as our ship pulled in to dock. Where would I connect for my carriage ride to the Mountain House? Would the porter get my bag off the ship and bring it to me before the train left for the mountains?

Being familiar with the necessities of survival in New York, worrying unnecessarily about such things was anathema to my usually confident character. The excitement of being out of my element ended when the overwhelming discomfort of a new experience set in. I reminded myself that I chose to take a long trip to the mountains to experience something new and get my head out of numbers on paper.

I patiently waited with others and walked the gangplank from the ship to the dock. A wooden overhead arch with scroll work painted "Catskill Landing" greeted us when we stepped on land. I tipped the porter, who looked very professional in his white coat and embroidered "Hudson River Day Line" on the breast pocket, as he brought my bags from below deck.

The dock was solid but worn and could have used a little repair, but mostly new paint. This defined much of what I observed in Catskill. Most of the city seemed locked in time, but not everywhere can be as modern and sophisticated as New York.

Comforted in my pretentiousness, I was bombarded by a pushy boy to buy a local paper. Surprised by his brashness but encouraged by his tenacity, I purchased his paper and gave him a tip. The paperboy gave me a genuine, "Thank you," and an even more genuine smile. I thought it appropriate to ask him where I might catch the train to the mountain house.

He pointed with not a moment's hesitation to a sign on my right clearly labeled "Catskill Mountain Railway Depot". I felt sheepish that one moment I was rewarding myself for my obviously more sophisticated life, only to be corrected by an upstate paperboy.

The Catskill Mountain Railway

A Catskill Mountain Railway Locomotive stopped at the Otis Elevating Railway Junction Station with the Catskill Mountain House high up the Great Wall of Manitou

I hoisted my travel bags and did my best not to appear to struggle with my possessions. Another young man approached me in a sharp, blue and grey suit with "Catskill Mountain Railway" embroidered on his crisp jacket. With evident sincerity he said he wanted to help.

He grabbed my bags with gusto, and I followed him the few steps to the depot where I recognized other fellow ship passengers.

I tipped the fine young gentleman well, purchased a ticket at the rather rudimentary ticket window and boarded the train. I considered myself fortunate to find a comfortable window seat. Small talk with fellow passengers filled the brief gap in time until the train left the station.

As we started moving very slowly out of Catskill Landing, we passed through a small tunnel and emerged on the other side of the main thoroughfare. Out my window I observed elderly people sitting on porches waving, children running, and a boy moving a hoop with a stick down the other side of the street.

The same two-story buildings I could see from our ship now looked even more similar, with one or two balconies in the front and at best four windows across. Brick and wood facades needing painting abounded. The churches had immaculate flower-covered grounds and bright paint. We rolled out of town away from the waterfront and toward the line of foothills left and right ahead of us like a mountain blockade.

We parted from the buildings that lined Main Street in Catskill and headed for the mountain ridge which loomed larger with every mile. Curving our way past small houses and fields of vegetables, hedgerows separating hay fields and fenced animals, over steel trestles and perilously close to rock outcrops the swaying train entered the woodlands.

Tree branches filtered speckled sunlight on our railcar. Occasionally we would break out of the trees and pass bucolic fields of carefully planted crops. I struggled to identify the plants growing in the different fields and marveled at the uniform rows that were spaced and lined up so perfectly as to maximize growth and efficiency. As we passed those fields, I was momentarily lulled by how the rows lined up in such a way it reminded me of rows of numbers. I reasoned this was a reminder why I was on vacation.

The conductor entered our railcar. An older gentleman, he wore the same blue and grey suit with "Catskill Mountain Railway" on his jacket like the suit the enthusiastic young man wore earlier. His badge clearly said "Conductor" and his pronouncement style and self-assuredness let us know he was in charge.

"About one hour to Palenville. We pass through Leeds, South Cairo, and stop at Cairo Junction. Only bluestone and hay take the train from Cairo Junction to Cairo. All passengers going to Cairo or South Cairo exit at Cairo Junction and take a carriage. All passengers going through to Otis Junction or Palenville stay on board. Tickets please."

I handed him my ticket and he punched it perfunctorily and moved on down the railcar. Amazed at his sure-footedness as we rocked through the countryside, I took a quick look at his shoes and noticed they needed to be shined. As accountants, we try to be well-dressed and well-groomed to maintain an air of economic stability for our clients' trust.

Also, to be fair, one is never very far from a shoeshine boy in New York City. Trying to leave my pretentious, judgmental "New Yorkers know best" attitude behind, I could not help opining that his shoes were a bad reflection of the railroad business with which he was associated, prompting me to mumble,

"What possible purpose is a conductor on such a short train?"

As the train was obviously a narrower gauge than normal, the small interior pushed riders together closer than comfort. An attractive woman to my right heard my utterance and said she understood that kids were sneaking on the train, taking free rides, and were causing problems with the passengers.

"Even if caught they could walk back to Catskill from Palenville before sundown," she said.

I thanked her for the information and hoped we might have another chance for discourse. We continued to rock back and forth as we snaked through the woods and fields. The conductor announced we were passing through Leeds and South Cairo and reminded those who were going to the Mountain House to stay on board. After our stop at Cairo Junction the train took a decidedly different approach. The mountains were then to our right as we appeared to take a southerly route toward Palenville.

We followed a meandering river as we skirted along the bottom edge of the Catskill Mountains past small quarries, lumber yards and farms. The afternoon sun was now completely blocked by the mountains, and it seemed darker than it should for the time of day.

The conductor strode through our railcar again with much purpose spouting, "Next stop the Mountain House Station, then Otis Junction. Twenty minutes to Palenville."

Realizing that was my last opportunity to decide to stay on board and take the Otis Elevating Railway to the Mountain House or take a carriage, I deliberated my situation. Wishing I could see the Otis Elevating Railway before making my important travel decision, I told myself that I had made the decision already to take the carriage road and should follow through.

Rip Van Winkle Hollow

The Rip Van Winkle Tavern

I stepped off the train at the Mountain House Station, tipped the porter, grabbed my bags, and approached the dark building with a low-hanging porch roof and ornately carved shutters on every window that I assumed was the toll booth. It was also the only building in sight.

As the other train passengers struggled with their luggage toward the booth, I noticed they were an interesting mix of individuals. Maybe the long carriage ride would afford me the opportunity to ask them why they also chose the carriage ride, I pondered.

After answering a few questions, I purchased my ticket from a rather surly woman at the ticket window. I attached the luggage tag she gave me to my baggage, and then waited patiently by the carriage situated in the shade of the toll booth. I noticed there were four horses that looked exceptionally fit and well kempt. The carriage was well worn but equally well maintained by my observation.

A relatively short but obviously strong young man with curly blonde hair falling all around his ruddy face introduced himself as Greg and grabbed my luggage. After a quick exchange of pleasantries, he heaved my bags into the back of the carriage. I renewed my conviction and said I was interested in a more "country" experience. His lack of affirmation of my decision did not help my disposition.

An elderly woman in a slightly tattered but obviously expensive burgundy dress, a burly and somewhat well-dressed young man, and a young, quiet couple joined our excursion. As the last one to board I observed Greg help the passengers step into the carriage compartment, organize the luggage, strap the back compartment up tightly, and then check the horses and their bridles. After one last time circling the carriage for inspection, Greg came around to the door side again.

I was impressed by his thoroughness but also concerned this was all necessary due to the particularly stressful ride we were all about to encounter. Holding the door, Greg offered to help me into the carriage but noticing my height he offered that a seat with him up front might be more comfortable. Thinking this might enhance my "rustic" experience I took him up on his offer.

Tiny steps led up to the front seat, and I struggled to get my footing. I grabbed the side handle of the carriage for support and although I am a large man, I was surprised by the amount of sway I produced. It was not like the sturdy but hard riding carriages of the city, but rather a carriage made to conquer rough mountain roads.

I deduced the suspension of the carriage was a product of the different ride necessitated by mountain roads, but I was also concerned it was the result of wear from those same roads. I settled in the bench seat next to Greg, trying to get comfortable on the bench board.

With a quick "HE-YAA" and a snap of the reins, we moved with purpose down the dirt road toward the wall of mountains in front of us. I must admit the streets of New York are not particularly smooth, but this mountain road was very rough - muddy, rutted, with rivulets of grooves running in all directions as if the rain goes where it chooses. However, the ride did not seem to bother Greg, even a smidgen.

My back was already starting to tighten up as we moved closer to the steeply rising edge of the mountain ridge. We stopped suddenly and I grabbed a handle on the carriage side for stability. I was startled by the suddenness but pleasantly surprised as a small flock of sheep crossed the road in front of our carriage and sauntered down a path near the road into a meadow.

The sheep bleated quietly as they were led with intense purpose by a young girl in a simple white dress, with an even more intense, purposeful look on a black and white dog nudging the sheep along. A flock of sheep would certainly be an anomaly on a New York Street. I comforted myself that the trip would continue to introduce me to new and hopefully beneficial experiences.

We passed a field of cows so close I could see the hay in their mouths leaning over the fence toward the road, biting off longer hay afforded them there. Being so close to such a large animal was familiar, obviously due to horse carriages being so common in New York. For reasons of unfamiliarity, I was somewhat uncomfortable riding so close to a cow, so I pulled back slightly in my seated position. This lack of comfort was amusingly noticed by Greg and a small smile crossed his face. Up until now he spoke very little; he said,

"Never seen a cow sir?" to me with a slight sneer. As if the "sir" hid his contempt for city people and their lack of country knowledge and compensated for his smirk.

"Any animal that large without any constraints such as these horses have makes me a little nervous, so yes," I said.

"Being in a field with several cows would make me concerned for my safety as I would not want to be trampled by such a beast," I offered to explain my position.

"Cows don't trample people; they're dumb as rocks," Greg said.

"However, my brother t'was between two cows in a barn and the floor let loose. He fell, the cows fell too, and the cows helped break his fall. But the manure pile at the bottom was really what saved 'em. No bones broke or nothin'. All were good after all that," he said with conviction as if he saw it happen himself.

A brief break in the trees and a series of small meadows in the distance afforded me a look at the Otis Elevating Railway cut straight up the mountain to our left. I marveled at the sheer height of the funicular railway. Certainly, a feeling of vertigo would overwhelm even the most stalwart, I comforted myself.

"Over 1,600 feet vertical in 10 minutes. Called an engineering marvel of today," Greg said, noticing my observation and obliterating the pronunciation of *engineering* with his garbled country accent. Still, I was impressed he remembered the statistics.

"Already seen less people takin' this carriage this year. The ticket booth lady Mrs. Schumacher ain't happy," he said.

The Otis Elevating Railway near the Otis Summit Station
and the Catskill Mountain House

Trusting his riding skills to best his grammar, we passed a single-story white house with black shutters on the left. Suddenly thrust into the deep shade of afternoon as we entered the heavily wooded mountainside, we approached a steep section of the road. This was, obviously, the beginning of the same steep climb I just observed for the Otis Railway - the beginning of the Great Wall of Manitou.

The horses jerked, and I was pleased Greg appeared seriously intent on getting us up the mountain without hesitation. Chomping their bits and tightening their restraints as we continued to climb slowly but with purpose up the mountain trail, the horses dug into the small red rocks of our steep but obviously better maintained road. We crossed a wide and sturdy wooden bridge spanning a creek running over bare rock.

Large, rounded-edged tan rocks defined the entire creek, and the water seemed to bounce downstream from one outcrop to another. A mist of water from the creek caught my nose and I could smell the cool, earthy odor of the water. The trail took a turn to the left and briefly followed the creek. Soon we stopped at a small, two-story building and adjacent barn on the right-hand side of the road. Greg noted that it was called "Rip's Tavern" and he needed to make a brief stop for the horses to rest.

A Catskill Mountains stream

As we had traveled a relatively short distance from the Mountain House Station to this "tavern", this duty could have been performed later to not inconvenience us passengers, I thought. Greg encouraged the carriage passengers to embark for a short moment and refresh themselves with a cool drink of spring water inside. As the interior of the carriage was as cramped, hot, and uncomfortable as most carriages, my fellow passengers disembarked accordingly. Greg again helped them out of their congested compartment as was not just his job but appeared to be his nature.

The elderly lady's perfume hit my nose before she passed me. Although the ride was noticeably rougher up on top, I considered my fortune as to not having ridden inside and having to inhale such a smell in a tight space. As we stepped up into the tavern as a group I turned and noticed Greg stroking the horses and speaking calmly to them. His gentle tolerance and exemplified manners made me feel a twinge of meanness for thinking so low of him.

The tavern was dark and smelled a bit musty. It could have used a good dusting, but we all wandered slowly toward a bar where there was, I assumed, the proprietor behind the structure. "Bar" was a grandiose term for this edifice, as it was as crude as it was grimy. We were all offered a (dirty) glass of cold water by a skinny man with dark, slicked-back hair and missing so many teeth he whistled when he spoke.

After briefly but thoroughly inspecting the water in the glass for unwanted visitors, I hesitantly drank while I closed my eyes to avoid seeing something unwanted on the glass edge. Before my last swallow of what was, admittedly, very cool and refreshing mountain spring water, I was startled by the proprietor's loud announcement that this tavern got its name because this was the last place Rip Van Winkle visited for a drink before his long slumber.

"Yup, we kept the room jus' the way it was when ol' Rip left. You can see it for 5 cents," he whistled with persuasion.

I now suspected and became conscious of the fact that the real reason we stopped was to line the pockets of the carriage company by deceiving the naive. Being aware that there are people like myself who understand Rip is a fictional character, I was also aware that there is a sufficient lack of sophistication among the multitudes to believe such a story and that Rip was real. Lastly, there is a percentage of the populace who are willing to forgo logic and five cents for a moment of indulgent fun.

Including myself in the last category, I offered a Liberty Head V Nickel, and he opened a door for me in the back of the tavern. There, as he had predicted, was a crude three-legged stool next to a table. The simple arrangement of a candle in a candlestick and a pewter mug in the middle of the table convinced me that my nickel was poorly invested, and this was not fun.

The proprietor then offered that, "Rip slept on a rock right up behind this very tavern. You can go see it if you like." I smiled, nodded politely in his direction but passed on visiting the rock.

As we walked out of the tavern to board the carriage, I attempted to converse with the young man riding alone with us who introduced himself as Harold Schroeder. He was politely responsive but somewhat detached in his temperament. As an accountant I work with people who run and operate all types of businesses and occupations. It is one of the most interesting aspects of my profession, and surreptitiously addressed my favorite childhood question - which was to inquire of one's occupation. Sensing his nervousness, I introduced myself, and asked him what his profession was in as nonjudgmental a voice as I could assemble.

"I am a salesman. I sell insurance," he said with little substantial evidence of conviction in his voice. Detecting his unsureness, I inquired of which company he represented.

"Poughkeepsie Business Insurance," he noted with more conviction in his voice this time, as if his attempted persuasion outweighed the fact that the business was assuredly not well known. "I plan to speak with Mr. Strand about insurance for the Mountain House," Harold said.

I wished him a sincere offer of good luck, and after the horses were ready, we departed Rip's Tavern. I assumed my original position next to our driver, and after checking the carriage and baggage we moved again up the mountain road.

"We'll take a short break soon after we get over the top of Dead Ox Hill," Greg said moments after taking control of the carriage again.

I wondered sarcastically to myself if there was another tavern of excitement at the top of that hill. Before I could finish the thought, Greg uttered, "It's for the horses. After that we head straight up to the hotel."

The horses dug in as well as they could to the loose red rock covering exposed solid rock underneath. My knowledge that we had been steadily climbing was confirmed as I looked to my left through the trees and was pleasantly surprised how far the valley appeared below. The excursion afforded me a view of the country from a bird's perspective, and I began to anticipate the famous view from the Mountain House.

My concentration was briefly but surely interrupted by a loud squeaking sound and the realization that the carriage had not only momentarily slipped but slid slightly backward. We were on a particularly steep section of the road and there were no loose rocks, just exposed rock that afforded little traction. My gaze quickly shifted from the valley to Greg's face, which was more determined than I had previously viewed.

A quick snap of the reins and we were moving forward, but not before there was a significant jerk of the carriage and its contents - including the passengers.

"We've had some rain and the rocks get slippery. It can be a tough ride sometimes. Worst is the rain," Greg said. I wondered if this was the spot where the ox met its maker.

"Everything all right up there?" said a female voice from inside the carriage. "

"All is good ma'am," Greg said as he leaned in toward the carriage compartment. Suddenly I noticed the road took a sharp turn to the right. I was overcome with anticipation that I might have to take the reins as Greg was not facing forward and we were perilously close to heading off the road. My fears were unfounded as Greg quickly repositioned himself, slowed us down and negotiated the sharp turn.

"That was Cape Horn. Next is the Short Level." Calming myself, I asked with sincere curiosity if every turn and stretch of this road had a name.

"This road been here so long it's mountain history. So many years - 'gotta lend itself to stories and names," Greg said. I admired his common sense. We continued our steady ascent and I again marveled at the altitude we had achieved.

Now the fields and farms were much smaller squares of green and brown than I had observed from the river. Buildings and roads were now difficult to discern. It all appeared as a blanket of colorful, rolling, beautiful landscape. Further affirmation of our height achievement was verified by the heavy breathing and sweat of our reliable horses.

At the next sharp bend to the left we stopped at a small, flat rest area. "Last stop before the Mountain House," Greg announced as he pulled the carriage to a flat area just off the main road and stopped next to a circle of rocks with burnt wood inside. Such a fireplace seemed risky in a wooded area, and must embers fly and catch the woods on fire I wondered? Surely, I surmised, that such a fire would be started only in the dire circumstance of an emergency.

Moans of displeasure could be heard from the carriage compartment as the occupants once more squeezed out of their confinement. Greg perfunctorily helped each person down the simple step and onto the rocky but level ground. The view from this small clearing did not go unnoticed.

"Quite the vista," I said to Mr. Schroeder, hoping to work my way to why he did not take the Otis Elevating Railway.

"Lovely," he replied, breathing in the mountain air through his nose as a smile crossed his expression. He then lit a cigarette.

I figured the best way to obtain the answer was to ask the question.

"Why didn't you take the Otis Railway?" I asked in as curious and unchallenging a manner as I could collect.

"My company didn't want to pay the extra travel cost. They're covering much of my expenses for the next three days. I have produced well for the company, so this vacation is an incentive reward." As I should have expected from my profession, it all came down to money.

Greg occupied his time tending the horses. Curious, I inquired why the horses did not get water during the breaks.

"It could kill them. I can't give them water until almost an hour after we stop at the mountain house," Greg said.

I did not pursue the topic further, as I have little knowledge of such things. I stretched, breathed deeply the mountain air, and enjoyed the view as I observed every other passenger was also. The quiet young couple was arm-in-arm standing nearby with their backs to us, quietly talking to each other and enjoying the view. Politely, I left them to their time together.

Slowly I approached the elderly female passenger. She was standing alone but with a pleasant smile on her face. I did not have a chance to talk with her at the tavern. She could not have played "hide and seek" as I could have found her in the dark by her perfume, which confronted my nose as I approached her and introduced myself.

"Caroline Miller. Pleased to meet you," she replied.

"Have you previously visited the Mountain House?" I inquired, as I got a better look at her deeply lined face. Her hands were slender, and her fingers were long. She had a pleasant, confident personality I found refreshing. I told her I was an accountant in New York and asked what business she pursued.

"I also worked in accounting, for my husband's business. He was a prominent clothier - from New York City also." Fascinated, I inquired further. "It is the Miller Clothier Company, and he was quite successful. I live in a flat on the Upper East Side. I can see Central Park from my windows. The company is run by his brothers and other men. I just collect a sum from the profits now. The classic rich widow," she said as she laughed a little at her self-deprecation.

"I heard you ask the insurance man why he chose the carriage road over the Otis Railway. I personally have affection for this road and came this way with my husband for years. It brings back good memories of our time together. It is also not rushed. I seek a different pace when I come up here," she said, accurately sensing my curiosity and probable inquiry. I thanked her for her time, and we parted agreeably.

Greg announced it was time to leave. The couple, still arm-in-arm, slowly walked back toward the group as we all headed back toward the carriage. Greg asked, as was his discretion, if anyone wanted to ride up top with him. I assumed that meant I would be stuffed in the carriage compartment for the rest of the journey. Fortunately, everyone assumed their original location and we were back on the road for the final segment of the excursion.

"Featherbed Hill," announced Greg, as we slowed our ascent and the horses seemed to relax however slightly. Now the view of the valley below shifted to our right as we had switched back to ascend such heights. The road narrowed and the edges of the road became more vertical.

This was a particularly difficult section of the road and I found myself gripping the side of the carriage once more. Greg's concentration subdued my reservations but not my displeasure with such a risky journey. My back was beginning to stiffen and was getting sore. We took a slow but discernable turn to the left.

"Long Level," Greg said, and we seemed to be on a particularly level section of the road.

Long Level, Rip Van Winkle Hollow

Because the trees around the road were beginning to level off, I assumed we were close to the "Pine Orchard" location of the Catskill Mountain House of which I had heard so much. After a few minutes I could see in the distance, on the cliff up and to the right of our road, the Catskill Mountain House. The white building and large front columns of the hotel seemed to protrude out of the wilderness as if to establish a distinct prominence over the surroundings.

We passed people leisurely walking the road which also indicated we hadn't far to travel. Overridden by a feeling of relief this journey would soon end, my previous thoughts on evaluating the merits of this carriage ride over the Otis Railway would now be forever folded and sealed with a wax stamp, by my observation.

Slowly passing the Otis Summit Station at the top of the elevating railway, my misfortune was to watch several people comfortably disembark from the Otis rail cars with smiles and happy chatter. That was not our condition. As our carriage passed the station and the junction with a railroad line, we approached a long wooden walkway and stopped.

"Welcome to the Catskill Mountain House. There will be a wagon here in a few minutes to take you to the hotel. If you desire, it is a short walk to the hotel," as he pointed to a nearby ascending path. "I'll bring your bags shortly," Greg announced.

Appalled that I might have to walk to the hotel up an incline, however slight and covered with a canopy of trees, to get to my destination I challenged Greg. Frustrated, I spouted,

"Walk? I can't see the hotel from here. You want us to walk?" But Greg simply nodded his head.

"It's for the horses. They must rest after such a trip, sir." Greg said in a manner that told me he was not at fault. The horses were sweating and breathing very heavily when we arrived at the walkway.

"I'm sorry. I'm just a little tired and sore." I placed my hand on his shoulder and said, "You did a fine job young man." The other passengers concurred.

The widow Miller reached in a fine, red velour coin purse and tipped our driver. Feeling uncomfortable for my outburst, I too tipped Greg who then proceeded to unhitch the horses.

The Catskill Mountain House

The front of the Catskill Mountain House

The younger members of our carriage chose to walk to the hotel. Mrs. Miller and I waited several minutes for the wagon then we also decided to walk to the hotel. She took my arm to steady herself and strode with conviction as we walked past large rock outcrops, some of which I observed were used to anchor the Otis Summit Station buildings.

As we walked up the steady incline I could hear and see water trickling out of the rock crevices to our left, where large trees with exposed roots barely gripped the fern and moss-covered rocks. A steep downward slope to our right led back toward the lakes which were barely visible through the trees. Competition for sunlight was intense everywhere in the woodland, as smaller trees vied for the limited amount of nourishing sunlight that trickled through the leaves from the larger trees that dominated the forest.

We merged with fellow hotel patrons wandering up the gravel-covered walkway. The path ascended a small hill and passed through a grove of pine trees that blocked our view of the hotel. The lack of activity from my sedentary occupation made conversing with my fellow strollers near impossible.

The trail leveled off and the trees became sparse as the trail bent sharply to the left. Steel buckets filled with water lined the back of a horse cart, and nearby a man filled containers from one of two well pumps extending above a wooden platform near the grove of trees. The walkway merged with a blue flagstone path as it opened into a very large flat field of exposed rock and short gold-colored grass.

Game courts, barns, gardens, and other buildings could be seen in the near distance to our right; the hotel was further to our left. As we approached a circular drive and passed between two stone pylons at the back of the hotel, the immensity of the structure revealed itself. We continued walking on a stone path toward the hotel as the afternoon sunlight shone on the back of the large white, three-storied structure.

A few large trees shaded the final section of the flagstone walkway near the back central entrance. Four large, two-story columns framed the open portico above us. Each round column had several straight, vertical grooves their entire length that ended with ornate, impressive floral carvings at the top. Mrs. Miller and I checked in with a pleasant young woman who identified herself as Madelyn at the office to the immediate right of the entrance.

Mrs. Miller grabbed my arm and thanked me for helping her along the walk. I assured her it was my pleasure as she said she was going to rest in her room. We said our goodbyes as I waited in the office for Madelyn to finish some paperwork. A small dog rested on a blanket on the floor, behind her office chair. He was an endearing dog with a black back, brown face and legs, and white on his chest.

I could see straight down a large, wide hallway toward the front of the hotel and my first glimpse of the famous view. After getting checked in and assured my bags would be in my room, I walked down the hall toward the famous portico. Reminded of the fact I had not eaten in hours, the bar and kitchen to my left surrounded me with scents of cooking onions, beef, and other imagined delicious delights.

A large, colorful floral pattern on the walls imparted a cheery ambiance. Fresh, fragrant boughs of pine were wrapped around parts of the staircase, and some hung randomly on the walls. Sunlight came through the top of a large circular stairway, and a sign pointing left labeled "Dining Room" was one I wanted to recall.

A young man with his arm around an attractive female sitting in a small foyer to my right gave me the impression he wanted everyone to admire his comely companion. Smiling black servers on either side of the portico entrance had their hands out to take change and offered to clean my porch chair. I offered that I was going to walk and did not require their assistance but tipped them well just the same as any good New York City resident would do to ensure good service, then or later.

I strode upon the portico where a few patrons were standing, smoking, and talking or simply rocking in chairs alone or in small groups. Two elderly gentlemen were playing a game of checkers. The long porch was several feet above the ground providing a prominent valley view. The front of the portico was divided into thirteen columns identical to the four pillars above the hotel rear entrance. The two-story columns were separated by a porch railing and balusters equally impressive in their fine, consistently curved woodwork.

The hotel was perched on a remarkable cliff facing east with a view of the Hudson Valley below in full unobstructed splendor. The immensity of it all took a few moments to fully appreciate.

Clouds like cotton balls suspended in the deep blue sky, extended like a canopy over the landscape as far into the distance as one could see. Shadows moved slowly over the waves of nature's summer colors which were separated by the thin, silver line of the Hudson River at the bottom of the valley far in the distance. The vastness of the view must include miles of visible terrain, I ascertained.

I stepped down the wide stairs located in the middle front of the portico which ended on a wooden walkway. Children were playing, people walking, and well-dressed young women were twirling their sun parasols strolling with equally fashionably attired and attentive young men at their sides. A popular locale for recognizable reasons, I estimated at least one hundred people were within my view.

The narrow wooden walkway that spanned the length of the hotel front and an iron railing separated everyone from the rocky precipice. Young women obviously employed by the hotel -

recognized by their identical, light blue dresses with neat white trim - were doing their best to discourage young people from playing on the railing, or beyond.

Having surveyed my immediate surroundings sufficiently for now, I reminded myself that the valley view would not be temporary. Feeling hungry and somewhat gritty, I found my way up the central staircase to my room on the third floor. The door lock appeared worn and the wood around the keyhole was scratched as if by a person blind with drink. I turned the smooth, round, white porcelain handle and was pleased to see my bags in the modestly furnished room.

The front of the Catskill Mountain House

The bed, chair, chest of drawers, nightstand and small desk were all simply made but sturdy in construction. Wide, dark wooden floorboards were occasionally covered with colorful braided throw rugs. A tall, mirrored wardrobe against the wall disguised a convenient, portable fold-down bathing tub I opted to have in my room. Much natural light entered from an open court in the center of the hotel wing. I wondered if a room with a view out the front toward the valley would have been worth the extra cost.

A paper placard greeted me on my nightstand. "Welcome to the Catskill Mountain House Hotel – The Grandest Hotel in the United

States!" it boldly proclaimed. Further perusing the paper, I noted it contained Dining Room hours (appropriate attire required), information about organized events such as game nights and tournaments, poetry readings and music evenings.

Another smaller paper listed options to choose a time necessary for the bath preparation, any special housekeeping needs I might have such as laundry, ironing and such, preference for scheduled room cleaning, and an odd mention of "The hotel room lights will be dimmed at 10:00 PM for our patrons' consideration and comfort."

A final piece of paper noted, "Respectful of the religious choices of our hotel patrons, by checking the preferred religious service we will do our best to provide transportation to such service." It listed, in alphabetical order, "Baptist, Catholic, Congregationalist, Episcopalian, Evangelical Methodist, Quaker and Other." I wondered where the carriage to the "Other" service went.

Anxious to meet and speak with fellow hotel patrons in the comforting, relaxed atmosphere of a good meal, I poured water from a pitcher and washed in a slightly chipped but functional porcelain basin. The hard, square, light green soap provided smelled like the hotel boughs and pine grove through which we had earlier walked.

Opening my bags, I discovered my evening jacket was quite wrinkled and convinced myself it did *not* smell like the worst part of horses from its carriage journey. I sprinkled some cologne on myself and joined others descending the stairs walking toward the dining room. Without the slightest exaggeration I can account for the fact that everyone was in a jolly mood.

Whatever the reason - their knowledge the meal would be well above average, the hotel accommodations afforded such contentment or a combination of niceties beyond my limited experience - it pleased me to be in such an atmosphere.

Seeking beyond prosaic discourse such as, "Do you stay at the hotel often? and "Where are you from?" I hoped to glean ideas for appropriate, stimulating, and topical conversation themes from my fellow patrons. As I listened intently, I noticed almost everyone was deliberating the natural beauty surrounding the hotel. The trails, beaches, tennis courts and view from the portico led discussions.

Reaching the first floor we entered the dining room filled with the din of hundreds of voices amplified by the expanse of this very large chamber. Against the middle of the long wall stood an indoor well of sorts, defined by several ladles hanging above a large bowl of water. The dining hall was close to the front portico, and I assumed without much deliberation that this encouraged patrons to help themselves to frequently refreshed cool water in the well and not disturb the staff and kitchen crew for a drink.

Divided lengthways by columns, the dining hall had the now ubiquitous pine boughs around each post. Tall trees in pots were positioned between windows and tastefully incorporated the surrounding forest into the hotel. Everyone took their seats at one of several tables that sat approximately thirty diners each. It appeared there were at least a dozen such tables, meaning the dining hall could easily seat over three hundred on my estimation. As no one seemed particularly determined to sit near (or not near) anyone else, we filed in similar to filling the pews at a busy church service.

"Have you eaten here before?" asked a portly, red-faced older gentleman to my left, having barely warmed my chair.

"I have not. Although I understand that the hotel is well noted for its culinary delights," I replied, anxious for more conversation.

"Where are you from, sir?" I asked, realizing I just committed the mundane question offense I was determined to avoid.

"I live in Hudson – just across the river and a little north of Catskill. It is a quiet but nice town. I'm a distributor, shipping and delivering goods of many kinds all over the Hudson valley. Name is David Baumgartner." he said as he shook my hand with his large, soft hand. I introduced myself and stated my occupation.

"Everything is served boarding-room style; take some from a plate and pass it on. You are in for a very good meal my friend. No one leaves this table hungry. They stick close to the menu. Kippered herring on Sundays only," he said with more than a smidgen of anticipated delight.

"So, the kippered herring is good?" I asked, continuing our exchange.

"Wonderful." he said, with the conviction of a hefty man's favorite food.

At that moment, the doors of the connected kitchen abruptly swung open and several black men wearing white jackets and gloves burst into the room. Some people gasped in delight as the servers carried large, blue-patterned dishes of food to different sections of our table. Serving spoons and ladles were provided, and as soon as the dishes were placed on the table patrons politely helped themselves and passed the dishes in the way described. Dish after delicious dish of food was presented including steak, lamb, and ham; cold meats including tongue; cheeses, bread, fruit, and cake.

Eggs and potatoes prepared every way possible were presented with the other dishes in an orderly and professional manner. And, of course, the kippered herring. The surrounding natural beauty and view were the reason many were drawn to this hotel and this setting. But the food was also understandably an important factor why patrons were willing to make such a trek.

Based upon our limited conversation between eating and passing food, I gleaned that the woman to my right and her husband beside her were the Romanos from Philadelphia.

"Italian dishes are my favorite," I said, noting that great Italian restaurants proliferate in New York City. He said his mother was a remarkable cook from Italy. The couple also expressed their appreciation for the effort the hotel kitchen crew and general hotel staff made to please the patrons. It was why they have returned to enjoy many summer sunrises and sunsets here.

"Consider asking for a candelabrum from the staff in the evening. You'll experience this hotel in the classic manner," Mrs. Romano offered. I thanked them for their conversation and advice, finished my cake and coffee, bid good evening to my dinner guests, and headed toward the stairs.

Having pleasantly immersed myself in two of my favorite pastimes - eating and talking, I briefly considered sitting on the portico and seeking more conversation. Tired from my long trip and sore from the carriage ride, I decided to take the stairs to my room and rest on the bed. I woke slightly confused by my unfamiliar surroundings. A couple of hours had passed, and the room was getting darker every minute.

Still in my clothes and shoes I shook myself awake enough to find my way to the light switch and the dim light reminded me that it must be after 10:00 PM. Believing that my rest would afford some reading time, I remembered that candelabras were an option for those who wanted them. Impressed by the well-lit hallways and stairs, I supposed this mountain house must look like a beacon of electric light from the valley below.

I descended the stairs to the first floor and asked an employee where to get candles for my room. He pointed toward the kitchen, and as I entered the smells of our entire meal invaded my nose at once. Unfortunately, it was a slightly unpleasant smell, like a bad cook who gets the dish correct but then ruins it with a few more ingredients.

The kitchen was clean, but cleaning materials and a hint of decomposing waste from bins on the floor finished the kitchen *aroma*. It took some strength to continue my entrance. "May I have some candles?" I asked a stout chef with a full, impressive mustache as I steadied myself on a slightly greasy floor. His white kitchen apron and tall chef's hat were covered in stains, new and old. Other similarly outfitted kitchen staff were busy washing dishes, sweeping floors, and wiping down counters.

A small ice room lined one wall and when an employee opened it, I could see large blocks of ice fogging the inside. Several coal stoves were located against another wall. Each stove had an angled, black pipe extending through the outside wall for ventilation. The entire kitchen resembled hell from the intense heat of the stoves, and the sweat on the chef's brow was profuse.

"Here you are sir." the cook said in a hoarse, Scandinavian accent as he handed me a heavy, black iron candelabrum from a shelf above one of the stoves. It had three short candles stuck in the nozzles, and the drip pans were covered with wax. A quick glance at the other candelabras forced the realization they were all about the same. Not wanting to complain my first day at the hotel, I smiled and thanked the burly chef. However, two of the candelabras on the shelf were twisted and fused together in an odd fashion. I inquired about the strange object.

"I wasn't here," the cook replied, "but I was told that one evening a few years ago lightning came down through the center staircase and fused those candelabras together. How the hotel didn't burn is unknowable."

At that moment, the small, black and brown dog I had observed in the hotel office suddenly scurried into the kitchen. One of his front legs was deformed as he hobbled and listed slightly due to this malady, but seemed to get along in his endeavors just fine.

Just then I was surprised by the head cook yelling, "Sebastian! Get out of my kitchen!" with the slightest amount of sincerity, allowing me to interpret that Sebastian's nightly kitchen stroll was probably a familiar occurrence with the kitchen staff. I thanked the chef and returned to my room.

After some time, relaxing in my room contemplating my itinerary, I used the communal bathroom at the end of my hall which was old but serviceable. On my return I was interrupted at my room door by a young man who, without identifying himself and disavowing any form of introduction, asked me for any candles I might have. I inquired, in a pseudo-comical mocking tone, was he afraid to ask "Sven" the chef for more candles?

"Oh no sir." he replied in a respectful tone. "They only give short candles to discourage late night parties. We just want to play cards in our room this evening - have a little fun. May I have one of your candles?" he asked again, now with more angst than before. I wondered why I was chosen but determined there weren't many others yet awake.

I gave him two of my candles and he walked away with a smile that led me to surmise there were more than card games on his agenda that night. I comforted myself this was a common occurrence and hoped he would be responsible with his renewed sources of evening light. I reluctantly acknowledged I was too tired to read anything as I entered my room. After snuffing out my remaining candle, moonlight lit my way to the bed. The aches and pains from the day did not prevent me from falling immediately into a deep, fresh mountain-air slumber.

Desire for Companionship

Early morning view from the Catskill Mountain House

The muffled clang of a bell startled me from my sleep. In the dark of my unfamiliar surroundings, I barely awoke and was convinced I was still in my New York City dwelling. Certain that firemen were ringing bells outside my window, and I must evacuate immediately, I frightfully stumbled out of bed and rushed to the door to determine from where the bell sound came.

Slowly acquainted with my current surroundings, I was still gravely concerned about the alarm sound. One of the black servers was ringing a small bell as he walked down the hallway. As he passed my room, I hurriedly inquired what happened.

"Just lettin' people know it time to see da' sunrise," he said with a smile.

My heart still beating profusely, I determined an attempted return to slumber would be unrewarded. I dressed and walked down the stairs to the portico. Surprisingly, many people had availed themselves of the opportunity to observe daybreak. The air was cool, and a mist rose from the valley up the cliff and drifted around the mountain house hotel.

It was still dark, but the slightest hint of light was peeking toward us over the mountains across the valley on the other side of the Hudson. In places it appeared as if one could step off the precipice and walk across the valley on clouds. As more patrons shuffled onto the porch, they were politely quiet and there were hushed discussions as if this were a religious ceremony that must be respected. Everything appeared in orange light as the sun rose on our faces and the hotel. The warmth felt good, and I assumed it would be another hot July day even here in the mountains.

"Beautiful, isn't it?" said someone with a vaguely familiar voice to my right. I turned to recognize Mrs. Romano.

"Yes, it is quite impressive," I replied. "Sunrise on the front portico, sunset on the back portico," she offered.

As I looked slightly confused about the sunset reference I inquired further.

"Oh, yes, just through the French doors off the ballroom is a small portico that is just lovely for sunset viewing," she responded with the same friendly expression as at dinner. Appreciating her merry start to my day, I wondered if everyone from Philadelphia were as friendly.

I returned to my room and prepared for breakfast and my planned activities. A hike to Boulder Rock and the Hotel Kaaterskill was the focus of my plans. My memory of the kitchen did not deter my desire for more of their pleasant fare, as I reminded myself it was clean and all kitchens in the summer probably smell the same.

Breakfast was served in a manner like dinner with plentiful servings including fruit, oatmeal, and griddle cakes; fresh fish including codfish with cream, biscuits, rolls, cold meats, eggs, and potatoes. My breakfast companions were as polite as possible. I was bordered by a quiet and very polite young businessman from Albany, and an older gentleman who said he came to the Catskill Mountain House as often as he could afford. He seemed most relaxed and happy to be here, as did everyone with whom I had spoken.

Leaving the table after exchanging pleasantries with my morning acquaintances, I walked out on the portico and appreciated the view once again. The morning fog had long lifted away, and the true panorama revealed itself. No Thomas Cole painting captured the profound effect of standing on the edge of such a vista. Nor could anything of man's creation match such magnificence.

From as far left and as far right as one could see was God's colorful world on beautiful display. The sun shone off the barely visible silver sliver of the Hudson which divided the scenery miles in the distance. This perch on a cliff granted all who visited, a show to exceed all shows without any motion or activity, providing profound divine inspiration. Serenely peaceful and awe inspiring, I wondered why I considered a hike. "Why leave? What would I find to rival this expansive view?" I asked myself.

Young women employees of the hotel were again keeping watch on a few children as I walked along the boardwalk in front of the hotel. One of the children slipped from the grip and reach of one of the staffs' control and started to run. The child then tripped and almost landed at my feet. I reached out and caught the girl as she fell and lifted her up to confirm her condition was well.

She gave me an adorable peck on the cheek, and I laughed out loud at the sweetness of her gesture. Feeling slightly embarrassed by her obvious and sudden display of affection, I blushed. My experience with children was limited and on exhibition. A worker girl thanked me for my help and apologized for any inconvenience. I offered that there was no inconvenience, I loved children and was glad the little one was OK.

Concerned my embarrassment was noticed, I returned to the porch stairs and proceeded to walk through the hotel toward the back entrance hoping for a different perspective. As I passed the lounge close to the portico door, I noticed a man alone in a wheelchair. He was missing a leg, and by his age I assumed he was wounded in the Civil War. I engaged with him long enough to thank him for his service and chatted about my dad's experiences in the war.

"You would be a fine gentleman to bring me a cool drink," he said when asked if I could get him something. I proceeded to the dining room and brought a drink from the indoor well. He thanked me as I left, and we agreed to talk later.

Although not twenty-four hours had passed, my comfort with the surroundings pervaded a growing familiarity with the hotel as I continued my stroll down the hall, to the back entrance past the busy office and out the back entrance. Then, I first noticed her. She was pouring water from a metal bucket onto a bed of flowers beside the bluestone walkway.

Obviously, an employee by her work, she was a little older than the other white women I had so far noticed employed by the Mountain House. Her brown hair was pulled back, and she wore a simple dress, but oddly not a workers' garment. Attracted by her beautiful green eyes and soft looks, she passed a pretty smile to me; I assumed she was being polite as to all hotel patrons.

"I'm planning a walk to the Hotel Kaaterskill. Can you offer any suggestions?" I said, hoping my small talk would lead to conversation.

"I'll be going there later today to greet a friend. I can show you the way," she said with a peaceful countenance that furthered my attraction.

"Karl Debacher - pleased to make your acquaintance." I said as gentlemanly as I could assemble and offered her my hand.

"Elizabeth Jackson - pleased," she responded and took my hand gently in hers. An uncomfortable moment passed when we both looked each other in the eyes. "I'll be leaving after lunch. Does that time work for you?" she said as we gently withdrew our touch. I did not deliberate whether having an attractive woman as my hiking companion would be better than expectations.

"That would be fine," I said, trying not to sound too eager. "I will look forward to your company. Where is best to meet?" I asked.

"Here, near the office," she said. I agreed and moved enthusiastically toward the front portico to decide how to occupy my morning with activities until our walk.

Should I reengage my discussion with the veteran? Take a short walk? Rest before the afternoon hike? These queries occupied my time as I wandered the grounds of the hotel. The weather cooperating, I decided to follow the signs to the lakes and beach areas. This led me to the backside of the hotel, through the stone pylons that defined the drop-off point for carriages from a circular drive; past the bocce and tennis courts, barns and other service buildings located behind a line of trees somewhat obscured from the hotel.

More signs led me to a boardwalk that twisted through the woods and ended at South Lake beach. As I walked out of the woods into a clearing, I observed the warm morning sun on the beach revelers, and I welcomed the idea of taking a cool swim after my afternoon walk. Sitting on a bench near the beach, I noticed that the lake had many large tree trunks around the shoreline, which vaguely detracted from the native beauty of the forest lining the water.

I found myself thinking about Elizabeth and how my afternoon might progress. Watching loving couples and their children play in the water, I was reminded that the longing to get married and have a family was always a desired outcome. I had heretofore enjoyed the pleasures of relationships with women, but long-term relationships had eluded me. Friends and an active social life gave me a satisfying existence.

But there was always the desire to find someone special and have a family that caused a slight disdain for my solitary life. Hidden by the dedication to my work, I could no longer suppress my desire to not be alone. Hundreds of people having a good time in the mountains may afford me an opportunity to meet someone special, I thought.

Would I ruin such prospects by associating with a hotel worker, I asked myself? My decision to put this situation in such a scenario was to justify my concern that Elizabeth was not interested, already had a beau, or would reject my advances should we get to that situation. My pretentiousness would not overcome my desire for companionship.

As I strode back toward the hotel, I reminded myself that I was going on a walk, and to be realistic about any anticipated romantic encounters during my visit. "Why so much pondering about a woman with whom I have hardly become acquainted?" I asked myself. Surrounded by the natural beauty of the mountains, open spaces, woods, and stunning vistas, my return walk reminded me to enjoy both the natural habitat and the friendly conversations to come.

Satisfied in my determination to have a meaningful and pleasurable trip, the likelihood of a romantic encounter was now realistically appreciated and prioritized appropriately. A sudden "toot!" of a train whistle gave me pause and enough time to see a train which just left the Otis Summit Station pass between the North and South Lakes to the excitement of the beach members.

Several "toots!" from horns and excited yelling came from a large passenger wagon stopped by the road and the railroad tracks between the lakes. Much waving ensued and the train gave one last quick blast as it headed up a small hill, through some trees and out of sight.

Although the carriage road and the train tracks crossed between the lakes together with ample room for both to pass comfortably, the wagon driver waited patiently while his nervous horses wrestled their reins and stomped their hooves until the train had passed. Colored streamers tied to the carriage flowed in the wind as the merry wagon riders tooted horns and hollered in fun riding between the lakes.

My attention was enticed by more activity on my return stroll. As I walked between the lakes and past North Lake beach, I observed three young men filling a hand pump fire engine. A hose was in the lake water, and the men were pumping a steel bar on the side of the engine to fill the tank. I was accustomed to witnessing similar fire engines in the city but had never seen one getting water.

"Haines Falls Fire Department" was proudly painted in big letters on the side of the red engine. More than a few women at the beach were distracted by the shirtless, sweating young men at their work. A carriage was unloading patrons at the stone pylons on the circular drive as I passed and continued toward the hotel. Two tennis games were underway despite the heat. Several men were enjoying a game of bocce, which seemed the appropriate warm summer game in the shade of two trees near the rear entrance.

I checked my watch as I entered the back entrance and gave a nod to the office personnel. "An hour until lunch," I thought as I walked through the hotel toward the front porch. As I strode across the portico and down the central stairs, I observed several colorful sun umbrellas in red, yellow, and blue, shading tables which lined the front of the hotel.

Numerous people were sitting at the tables as black men were hurrying back and forth taking drink orders to the bar for tips. An employee profusely thanked an elegant lady at one of the tables for what was probably a substantial gratuity. The vibrant sun umbrellas, dozens of adults, children, employees, the American flag high on a pole and an occasional dog all blended like a colorful living painting of life at the hotel.

People smiled as I passed them on my way to the South side of the hotel, where several young children were playing pretend Civil War games in an open field. Almost all of them were wearing kepis, an approximately equal divide amongst the children between the grey and the blue military hats. The kepis appeared free of wear and almost new. Shouts of "Take that hill", "Rebels!" and "Charge" from the children interspersed this odd scene of youthful bedlam and correctly colored caps on each side.

Although decades had passed since the war, I wondered if any patrons at the hotel might take offense at such a scene. Boys wrestled in the dusty grass to impress pleasantly dressed young girls in the shade of the house twirling their parasols and pretending not to watch the mayhem. On my return to the porch stairs, I nodded and tipped my hat appropriately to the many couples and others walking and sitting in front of the hotel. I returned to my room for a quick wash-up and changed into more appropriate hiking shoes.

Andrew at our office had strongly recommended I bring sturdy shoes and assured me it was worth the extra baggage weight. I strode downstairs, enjoyed the smells coming from the kitchen and reveled in the anticipation of more good food and interesting conversation during lunch. Because of its active conversations and somewhat crowded conditions I assumed without much proof that the lounge near the front of the hotel was a popular place to wait for the meal call. Its location close to the dining hall assured those in attendance a guaranteed early seating.

My reasoning concluded that since everyone was certain to secure a seat in the massive dining hall, these people wished to have conversation before the meal, as it is never proper to propel food on your fellow patron during discourse at the table. Of course, it occurred to me that my personal desire for conversation drew me toward an incorrect assumption. The more probable actuality was that these people loved to eat, and they perceived, obviously incorrectly, that somehow the hotel might run out of food.

Lunch was served in the way us patrons anticipated and did not disappoint. Differences in presentation dismissed my misperception of limited resources and rush to the dining hall. The food was already on the table and a more self-serve arrangement than breakfast or supper, with servers refreshing those dishes that dwindled. No large quantity of the mealtime was served hot, but there was the usual abundance and variety to keep everyone satiated.

Like dinner, sliced meats such as lamb, beef and tongue were presented on large plates as well as numerous types of fruit and cheeses. Every type of bread desired including Boston brown, rye, French and graham varieties were passed. Dessert included pound cake and ginger snaps. My young lunch companions to my left were less than enthusiastic to converse during the meal. Because of the limited interactions between them, I assumed it was nothing personal. The patron to my right was friendly and cordial, and our conversation drifted toward politics.

A relatively young man who said he was from Olive, NY, appeared to be alone and did not mention a companion. We had more than a little in common, as during our introduction we recognized we were both involved in financial and business professions.

"Have you heard that Cleveland might win a second term?" he said, noting the oddity of him serving two non-consecutive terms as President.

"It would be historic, but more importantly would send a message from businessmen such as us that the government is too big, and Harrison's policies have been unjustifiable. Ridiculous tariffs and excessive federal spending will put us all in a poorhouse," I said, hoping his experience and commonality in business would find him in agreement.

"Oh yes, I agree. Harrison has been a disaster for business. The 'Billion Dollar Congress' as they're known has spent recklessly," he concurred at the same time large bowls of fruit were being brought to the table. Soon people began to leave the dining hall and I offered my lunch companion that I would enjoy continuing our political discussions again soon. He nodded in agreement, and I made my way toward the back of the hotel near the office where I hoped to meet with Elizabeth.

She was just coming out of the office as I walked down the hall, and our eyes met briefly. She passed another pretty smile toward me.

"I'll be ready in a few minutes. My friend Eliza and I have Monday afternoons off, and we love to visit and walk together," she said with a soft, relaxed expression that reflected her life in the quiet beauty of the Catskills. "Also, today is Independence Day and there will be much excitement this evening when they light fireworks off the front of the hotel," she said, unable to hold back her child-like enthusiasm for the holiday.

Her combined presentation of pulled-back hair, simple dress and pleasant personality all continued to intrigue me. This was not a sophisticated city woman. Rather, this was a woman who was confidant and comfortable with herself and her environment.

"May I take lunch now Miss Liz?" came from a small young girl employee behind me.

"After the office is swept," said Elizabeth.

Her marital status now firmly confirmed, I fought my inner desire to make more of the information than it warranted. I walked out the back door and waited patiently for her to finish her obligations. Although understandably lacking the beautiful view from the front of the hotel, the surroundings of the back of the hotel were well arranged with flowers, small gardens punctuating the walkways and game courts, and shade trees with the occasional table.

Nearby, kitchen workers unloaded crates of meat, fruits, and vegetables from an ox cart as another crew unloaded ice from a horse cart.

"I get to drive the buckboard back," one of the barely teenage young men unloading the ice from the horse cart said firmly to the other young man.

The contrast of such hard work happening in the back of the hotel so that so many could have leisure on the front portico was interesting to witness.

Bear Scat and Boulder Rock

Boulder Rock and the Kaaterskill Hotel

"Have a nice afternoon, Maddie," I heard Elizabeth say toward the office as she strode down the hall in my direction. "I am ready to walk to the Hotel Kaaterskill, Mr. Debacher." she said as she stepped outside into the sunlight.

She placed a large sun bonnet on her head, and I noticed her pale, smooth skin. Avoiding the sun had given her a wonderful complexion. Not wanting to sound too forward, I avoided saying anything about her appearance, but continued to be intrigued by her attendance to her presence without the slightest pretense. I reveled in the refreshingly different simpler approach, so diverse from the stuffy environment of the city.

"Please call me Karl," I said to her.

"And please call me Liz," she said without hesitation.

"I would like to see Boulder Rock on our way if that is not too troublesome," I said, hoping it would fit in her schedule to meet her friend at the Hotel Kaaterskill.

"That would be nice. We can take the trail there and then pick up the escarpment trail to the carriage road," she said without reluctance, which affirmed it was not inconvenient to her day.

We both headed south toward the trail leading to Boulder Rock and the Hotel Kaaterskill. A gentle, warm breeze came up from the valley and caressed my face as I turned the corner of the hotel toward the wooded trail. Old Glory planted on a tall pole near the cliff edge, ubiquitous in virtually every brochure picture of the Catskill Mountain House, was furling and unfurling in the soft wind.

I roughly knew what direction to pursue based upon some rudimentary maps framed in the dining hall. Not much else was offered as far as road or trail maps to hotel patrons, the assumed reason being that there are always people walking and moving between the hotels so you will never be alone or lost.

Two lean, short black workmen in loose clothing were wielding big scythes, clearing the taller grass areas near where the children were playing their Civil War games earlier. Their swinging motion and grass cutting stirred up numerous hopping flying bugs; so many it looked like the ground was spewing them into the air.

Unable to discern a course of direction to avoid these creatures, one insect landed on my shirt just as we passed the workmen. I looked down at my chest near my face and observed the most hideous green insect with huge back legs climb on me for a moment and then it leapt off and flew away. Not wanting to seem flustered by a simple insect, it took every ounce of my fortitude to retain my composure in the moment.

I looked to detect a slight smile on one of the workers due to my inability to totally suppress my reaction. I was fortunate that Liz missed my abhorrence as she was slightly ahead of me leading us toward the small break in the trees where the path began.

As we entered the woods the character of the wilderness became whole to me. Suddenly, with just a few steps into the trail, the entire environment changed. Coming out of a sunny field into the thickly wooded forest was almost too much for my eyes to adjust. Momentarily adjusting to the much darker environment and dappled sunlight through the trees, I had to watch where to put my feet as we immediately began to climb up the trail over tree roots, large rocks, and muddy terrain.

As we continued to climb up the trail I wondered if the entire walk to the Hotel Kaaterskill would be as adventurous - and difficult. After a short climb I noticed the trail continued to twist and rise through the trees. More roots, boulders, mud, and the occasional flatter trail section where, not wanting to seem unhealthy, I could surreptitiously catch my breath.

Liz was fine with this environment, and I pleasantly observed she maintained the resourcefulness needed to adjust to both the refined environment of the hotel and the roughness of the wilderness. Occasionally, small trails cut to our left off our main trail, and I asked Liz if these would afford us the opportunity for unobstructed views of the valley.

"Yes, these trails lead to the cliff edge, and many have nice viewpoints. We can take the next one if you like," she said. As we took a left at the next similar junction Liz suddenly stopped and turned around with a slightly distressed appearance.

"We can take the next trail," she said, so I inquired why not this trail. "Fresh bear scat," was her simple but direct response.

I reconsidered if I wanted to take any side trail, and then realized quite quickly that we were in the bear's territory - not ours. *This* trail we were walking could be a bear trail as well as any other. I also realized I was way out of my comfortable city surroundings and felt more dependent on Liz's skills than I would have imagined when we left the hotel.

Continuing with the trepidation which replaced my relaxed demeanor, I reminded myself that the dreams I've had taming the wild would never come to fruition. James Fenimore Cooper's *The Deerslayer* hero Natty Bumppo, also called "Hawkeye," I am not.

"What other such beasts might we confront in this region?" I asked Liz, more than curious, if such close encounters with wildlife - especially large wildlife - are common here. Liz assured me such encounters are rare, and that bears usually run away if you shout as they despise loud noises.

"Sometimes in the evening the cooks must bang pots and pans when the bears get too aggressive while the staff load the garbage on carts for pig slop. Occasionally a raccoon will pop out from under the porch in the evening to eat crumbs under the tables and scare a guest, but I am sure most hotel patrons never see any wildlife, other than common birds and squirrels, during their stay," she said as we continued our walk.

We soon came to a trail junction with rudimentary signs, one pointing to the right for the Hotel Kaaterskill and another sign directing us forward toward Boulder Rock. I attempted to direct our conversation toward the more mundane as a distraction for my newly acquired respect for the wilderness. I asked Liz questions about our surroundings, such as the different types of trees in the forest. She was very patient as a teacher and had a natural relaxed method about her presentation in general and particularly in her speech.

"An Eastern Hemlock tree has two white stripes on the bottom of its needles," Liz said. "These trees were felled for their bark used in the local tanneries. You may have noticed large tree stumps around the lakes by the hotel. They were all felled, stripped of their bark and the wood left to rot," Liz said.

"What happened to the tanneries?" I inquired.

"All gone. Stripped the woods of the trees they needed for the business," she said.

A brief introduction to a few other types of trees stimulated my interest in learning more. She encouraged my interest in such knowledge as the distinctly different leaves, branch growth and bark of the trees which surrounded us. The sounds of many different birds chirping and calling became more apparent as we moved further into the woods.

While rounding a corner of closely spaced buildings in the city, I have been surprised by a gust of wind unforetold and stunned by its sudden intensity. But, in the open wilderness, I heard the breeze as it came through the trees in the distance and watched as the branches above us swayed gently in its influence. Even the wind seemed gentler in the country.

It appeared as if every tree responded differently to the small gusts of wind depending upon the size of its leaves, the number of its branches, and its height. Feeling more relaxed both in our surroundings and in our conversations, I asked her hopefully noninvasive questions about her employment - her schedule, duties, and staff responsibilities.

I explained that I was specifically interested in her work, and that ever since I was a child, I have been fascinated by the many different professions that abound. But I also strive to not pry with my curiosity. She acknowledged my concern and said she appreciated my interest as most patrons only converse with her or her staff when they desire something. She proceeded to expound about her work.

"I have worked at the hotel for three summers and this is my fourth summer here. "Herr Strand" as he prefers to be called, was a tough manager when I started here but he told me later it was to prepare me for my new position as supervisor. True to his word, my first year of work was generously rewarded with a promotion the second summer to supervising several young women who clean, help in the gardens, and serve the patrons' general needs. I work six and a half days a week, I get Monday afternoons to enjoy my friends and serve just myself," she said, adding a little upturn in her voice when she noted she was able to serve just herself for a few hours a week.

Attractive but not beautiful, I was more curious about her as we became more acquainted.

"With all the preparations needed for the fireworks show and more tonight I was pleasantly surprised Herr Strand let me have the afternoon free," she continued, increasing my curiosity about the evening's events. Not wanting to spoil the surprise, I did not inquire about the evening agenda.

The trail seemed to lead us over one mound then another but kept us basically at the same level. Soon we arrived at Boulder Rock, twelve foot long and ten foot tall perched on the edge of a precipice.

For the first time since arriving in the mountains I could see the Hotel Kaaterskill in the distance. I estimated we were at least a mile from the hotel, and I was quite astonished by the sheer size of the white edifice. It appeared one could fit three Catskill Mountain House hotels inside the Hotel Kaaterskill.

The Kaaterskill Hotel

The Kaaterskill Hotel

I thanked Liz for our short excursion on my behalf to see Boulder Rock, and we continued down wooden stairs that led to a narrow path near the cliff edge with signs that pointed toward the Hotel Kaaterskill. We passed fellow hikers and soon we connected with the escarpment trail which led to the beginning of a carriage road. A few carriages and their drivers were waiting patiently inside a small turnaround.

"Everyone has to walk from here to the Catskill Mountain House," Liz said, as if to answer my curiosity at this road ending in the middle of the woods. "The only way to get to the Catskill Mountain House Hotel by carriage from here is out the back of the Hotel Kaaterskill and between the lakes to the circular drive."

"I guess it was too difficult to build the road through this terrain," I offered, but it still didn't make sense to get this close and not finish the road. Thinking about the steep, rocky environment we just experienced gave affirmation to the appreciation for the lack of completion. The road was well maintained and level.

A few carriages passed us, and as we came closer to the Hotel Kaaterskill on our approach through the garden paths in front of the hotel, the truly immense size of the structure quickly became apparent. Hundreds of feet long, there was a larger, main hotel entrance section further from us. Several four-story tall pillars framed the main hotel entrance and long portico, which was also framed by a six-story tower on each front corner of the main hotel section.

A lower, four-story annex of the hotel was connected to the main section by a walkway between the second floors of the two structures. Liz indicated her friend worked behind the hotel, but I insisted on touring the Hotel Kaaterskill at least for a few minutes. She agreed but chose to wait on the front piazza.

Much larger than the Catskill Mountain House portico, it offered a serene view of the mountains and valley below, Still, despite having another smaller porch above the main portico which appeared to offer an even better view into the valley, it seemed compromised compared to the panorama enjoyed by patrons at the Catskill Mountain House Hotel.

Liz settled into a chair on the porch as I strolled into the main lobby. Advertised as the largest hotel in the world at over 1,100 rooms, this was an impressive hotel in every way. Whereas the Catskill Mountain House had a rustic charm with its floral-patterned walls and pine boughs, the Hotel Kaaterskill exuded elegance at every glance. Fine upholstered chairs, polished wood floors, exposed ceiling beams, arched doorways and opposing staircases on each end of the hotel reception hall all gave the immediate impression of opulence in contrast to the surrounding wilderness. Fine woodwork abounded. This was a hotel built to impress.

I noticed French doors leading to the dining wing which jutted out toward the back of the hotel. Upon opening the doors, I observed many well-dressed black men in identical white shirts, black pants and black jackets setting up for the next meal. Windows lined both sides of the elongated room which provided ample sunlight from each side.

Multiple exposed ceiling beams crossed the room and ended in round cornices between every other window. As each cross beam was visibly concentric into the distant, almost imperceptibly far end of the dining room, it further enhanced the reality that this was quite an extensive hall. The attention to detail continued here, with lines on the ceiling tastefully outlining the inside of each exposed beam section.

The dining hall had tables along each wall that held four patrons each, and a center aisle of tables which could hold six patrons each. White linen tablecloths, fine glassware, silverware, and flowers were placed everywhere to provide quite an elegant look. The plates had a simple but stylish blue scroll edge design.

Every table had its own server. "Little Neck Clam cocktail, Lobster Sauté Newburg, Breast of Chicken Madelaine, and Punch Amontillado" were on the menu I picked up from a table near the door. Because of the menu's fine delicacies and attention to detail, I was sure this was for the special occasion of the celebration of our independence that day. As I lingered more than I should during their preparation, one of the servers let me know they would be serving in about an hour and asked me if there was something he could do for me.

"No thank you," I replied, but further questioned, "Is this a special meal preparation today?"

He looked at me quite curiously and said politely, "No sir, this is how we prepare for every meal here."

As much as I appreciated the special attraction to the unembellished atmosphere of my hotel, this was a sophisticated preparation that I doubted ever graced the Catskill Mountain House.

I did not want to leave Liz alone on the portico for too long. Lobby signs indicated there was a Cigar Shop, Wine Room, Drug Store, and a Barber Shop in the Hotel Kaaterskill. My curiosity about the appointment of the rooms in the hotel now held a high interest to me. Alas, I resigned to the fact I would not get to explore further at this time and felt confident I could return for such pursuits on my own through the trails.

I walked back toward the portico and found Liz happily chatting with some of the hotel servers. Her comfortable charm and familiarity with the staff made her an attraction for conversation and attention at both hotels. She noticed me and politely ended her conversation with the workers. We walked around to the back of the hotel past the Icehouse and signs to the Steam Laundry. Several patrons were playing golf in open fields of green rolling hills that sloped away from the hotel. The stark openness of the posterior of the hotel contrasted sharply with the surrounding density of the forest near the front.

The south side of the Kaaterskill Hotel

We continued to walk away from the hotel and approached a large series of barns, a blacksmith shop and stables that could easily house over one hundred horses. We talked about the differences in the two hotels; Liz agreed politely but honored her profession and did not offer her opinion. I could smell the hay and horses as we approached the stables.

We walked out of the sunlight into a long, hay covered floor with an occasional horse's head protruding from the waist-high doors that lined both sides of the stable. Soon Liz introduced me to Eliza, who was brushing a horse. Eliza smiled politely and was surprised when I offered her a handshake, that gesture not being customary between patrons and hotel workers, especially black employees. She took my hand politely. Liz gently smiled.

"Mr. Debacher met ol' Bill at the Mountain House and gave him a drink of water," Liz told Eliza.

"Ol' Bill," Eliza concurred as if everyone knew him.

“One of my girls said she saw Mr. Debacher catch a little girl from falling," Liz also shared with Eliza, which now made me realize her interest in me was genuine. Without realizing it, I had impressed Liz simply by being myself.

Liz indicated she wished to visit her favorite horse named Ted near the end of the stable. Being sure Liz was out of hearing range,

Eliza turned toward my ear and said quietly "She likes you. She don't bring no hotel patrons down here, and 'spects you."

I watched as Liz hugged an especially friendly horse. At that moment, a tall, young man entered the stable and began talking with Liz. Not wanting to interrupt, I continued my conversation with Eliza.

"I find her country charm and easy mannerisms a refreshing difference from my city friends," I said as I watched Liz hug the young man. Failing to hide my displeasure of her obvious affection for him, Eliza politely chimed in with, "That's her brother, Pol. He works on the Esopus river most of the summer."

With an obvious exhale of approval upon hearing the news he was not a fellow admirer of Liz, I inquired of Eliza if she felt it would be appropriate to walk down and meet him. Surprised and pleasantly pleased to be asked her opinion, Eliza suggested it would be fine to do so. As I walked by the horse stalls to greet Pol, I noticed some horses poked their heads over the doors to greet me, while other horses were more reserved. I slightly chortled at the thought that most of my close experiences with horses had been inside a carriage and viewing only their backsides.

Liz turned to greet me and introduced me to her brother. A firmer handshake I had never experienced; Pol was quite tall and very muscular. I inquired of his duties.

"When the Esopus is running I ride down loaded ponies. When it's dry, I run ox carts up the mountain with store goods." he said, noticing my surprise as I imagined such a large young man dragging his heels on a small horse down a river!

"Are you saying you ride horses down a river?" I queried.

Liz offered, "A pony is a raft. Pol takes all kinds of things down the Esopus when it’s running. You've even taken bluestone down, haven't you Pol?" Liz asked, to encourage further enlightenment of Pol’s occupation and gliding past my misinterpretation.

"That's the crazy ride. Those stones are heavy so the Esopus must be running hard. Heavy ponies and a raging river are not easy," Pol said as Liz looked at the ground in an uneasy way. She was obviously worried about his dangerous work. "One of my friends..." Pol started to tell a story but Liz nervously cut Pol off before he started. A brief but uncomfortable moment later, Liz asked if Pol would be attending the evening's events at the Mountain House. Pol said he wasn't sure as his girl didn't like fireworks.

"Will you two be at the pavilion then?"

"Of course. She loves live music and dancing," Pol answered, failing to hide his excitement about that night's activities. I could sense it was time to start heading back as Liz said there were things to do at the hotel even on her day off. We said our goodbyes to Pol and Eliza and headed back out of the stable and into the bright sunlight.

A few Hotel Kaaterskill patrons were enjoying outdoor activities as we walked up a small hill toward the back of the hotel. Some were putting golf; other well-dressed patrons were playing croquet or bocce. The hotel continued a similar look as the front with a smaller wraparound portico that lined the first floor of the back of the hotel as well. Patrons sat in the shade of the narrow porch and watched as young women dressed in white nurse-like attire pushed covered perambulators along small footpaths.

Other similarly - attired women were watching young children behind a fence erected in the shaded back corner of the sizeable structure. As we rounded the south end of the hotel toward the portico, I looked north down at the front of the hotel as it stretched out in the distance and respected its immensity once more. I wondered if Liz wanted to talk with her friends at the Kaaterskill again. She had another purpose.

"Would you like some water? You must be thirsty after all this walking on a warm day," she said.

Pleased by another example of her continued kindness, I offered my thanks and said that would be appreciated. Knowing her desire to get back to the Mountain House, I was somewhat assured Liz would not spend much time at the Kaaterskill.

As we entered the foyer and Liz went into the dining area to ask for water, I was afforded another opportunity to observe the fine craftmanship and woodwork on display. We sat at a small table in the lobby and enjoyed our cool drinks together.

"Any other siblings?" I inquired, believing the query was not too invasive.

"Yes – a sister named Erin. She lives with my parents in Cairo." I inquired if Erin was also employed in the hotel business.

"Erin raises prize Angora goats on our small farm. Only three years raising goats and she won first place at the Dutchess County Fair," Liz said proudly and continued, "Angora goats are rather delicate and sensitive to cold weather. Erin sometimes takes our dogs to sleep with her and the goats in the barn on very cold evenings. Our dad didn't want the goats at first but was pleased when we received a hefty payment for the five pounds of valuable mohair each goat produces twice a year when shorn."

"Interesting. So, you grew up locally?" I asked, recognizing the name Cairo from my train ride.

"Oh yes, I'm a New York girl. But that means something different to you, being from the city." She offered, recognizing that us residents tend to use New York for the city moniker more often than for the state. "The mountains are my home; I grew up watching the sun set behind these hills all my life."

Several times during our conversation she smiled at me, which, combined with the positive review I received from Eliza, gave me confidence that she had genuine affection for me. I told her I was not married or had a paramour in New York. She seemed pleased to learn of my marital and romantic situation.

Herr Strand

The view of the Hudson Valley from the
Catskill Mountain House location

Although I still very much wanted to see how the rooms were embellished, I did not want to hold Liz from her duties at the Mountain House. Well-dressed patrons were playing checkers on the porch and children were chasing each other through the front gardens when we left the Hotel Kaaterskill and headed toward the Mountain House. Shadows were getting longer as slow-moving carriages shared the road with us. The carriages looped back where the road ended at the rocky path where the trails began. A sign pointed left toward the Mountain House Hotel or right toward Bolder Rock and Split Rock.

The distance to this location seemed shorter than our earlier walk; either familiarity or comfort with my surroundings was slightly affecting my judgement. Not forgetting our earlier potential meeting, I believed the sound of the carriages and horses would prevent an encounter with a bear. Now together in the woods for a second time, I felt my senses awakened but did not want to show my apprehension to Liz.

The rocks and tree roots roughly greeted my tired feet, and it seemed more difficult to traverse than our previous excursion. Working our way down the slippery trail, I wondered how I would find the energy to thoroughly enjoy the evening festivities. I fortified myself with the idea that a short rest and a bath may be my best plan before nightfall.

At one particularly tricky part of the trail we had to squeeze by a large rock that obviously did not cooperate with the path builders. At the same time, the trail sloped quite precipitously down the ravine. I stopped and offered Liz my hand in help. At that moment I realized she had consistently been much more sure-footed than my city skills had provided, but she accepted my offer and I felt comfortable with her touch. After we slipped around the rock and were on better footing, she smiled at me and touched my shoulder in appreciation. I smiled back and felt more comfortable with our growing affection than I had to the moment.

I heard children laughing as we worked our way down the rocky path toward the Mountain House, signaling we were close to our destination. The bright, late afternoon sun, to our left at the back of the hotel, cast the hotel's shadow onto the patrons strolling on paths and sitting at the tables and chairs in front by the porch.

The cliff precipice just a relatively few feet from the hotel was just too dangerous for inattentive and unattended children. Hence, the hotel had a small area on the south corner of the hotel with a low fence where small children could play safely while Liz's girls watched them. Liz stopped to talk with one of the young girls and picked up a little boy who seemed thrilled in her presence. Although I could not hear every word, the girls who worked for her spoke to her in a courteous manner earned by her easy manner and kind character.

As we continued to walk comfortably together past hotel patrons and guests, the excitement about this evening was evident. Palpable enthusiasm was demonstrated by loud talking and energetic guffawing. Liz stopped for a moment to greet and introduce me to an elderly couple sitting at one of the tables on the grassy area between the front of the portico and the pathway. Due to the growing revelry, I did not hear what she said. She was very brief, and I assumed it was just a greeting. We continued toward the stairs leading up to the front of the porch.

"They are the nicest couple. 'Been married forty-six years. Had five children..."
I interrupted with an exclamation of surprise at such a large family and said, "It must have been a lot of work..." when Liz uncharacteristically interrupted me and said, "None of their children lived past one year old. They finally gave up trying to have a family. The children at the hotel call her grandma. She loves them all and calls each one by name."

At that moment I turned to see the elderly gentleman reach across the table and place a small wildflower on his wife's dress. They smiled lovingly at each other, which convinced me that the love they had was very special to have survived such immense tragedy.

Barely able to compose myself from such a revelation, Liz excitedly grabbed my arm and said she wanted me to meet someone. We passed the steps to the portico on our left as we walked briskly at her lead toward a man sitting slightly tilted back in his chair near the iron railing, facing the valley. As we approached, I could see he was elderly with a short, full white beard and an intense expression.

He was wearing a black suit, black hat, white shirt, and shiny black shoes. It took me a moment, but I finally realized this was the famous Herr Strand who owned the Catskill Mountain House. Knowing his German heritage, I said, *"Guten tag Herr Strand,"* ("Good day Mr. Strand,"), and offered my hand. He returned with, *"Guten tag,"* and I interpreted by his sly smile that he appreciated my short excursion into the German language. He took my hand and surprised me with his strength.

"My name is Karl Debacher, and I love your hotel," I said as I attempted to sound as sincere as I could. "You obviously never tire of the view," I said, hoping to skip by the awkward attempt to convey my honest pleasure staying at his hotel.

"How could one tire of this," Herr Strand said with his deep German accent, as he swept his hand across the eastern horizon.

"Looks like a nice evening for fireworks and music at the pavilion," Liz said with a respect she obviously held for her old German boss.

"Thank you for your time. I must be going to see what I can do to help prepare for tonight," she added with more than a hint of excitement.

I offered an "*Auf Wiedersehen,*" ("Goodbye,"), to Herr Strand, to which he replied with a polite nod of his hat. Believing his hotel in good care, even on a revelatory evening commemorating our independence, Herr Strand comfortably returned to his tilted chair and grand view.

As we walked toward the porch stairs and were out of the hearing range of Herr Strand, I asked Liz, "Does he do much more than sit there?" Catching myself in possible rudeness as we started up the stairs, I interjected, "I meant, is he involved in the daily operations of the hotel?"

"He still commands attention to detail and insists on patron satisfaction as he has since he took over the Mountain House many years ago," Liz said. "He has always considered the 'Pine Grove' as he often calls it, a very special place," she added as we entered the main hall leading straight toward the back of the hotel and office.

Liz continued as I expressed interest in his story. "He shares his story with the staff every year at the beginning of our season. Even those of us who have heard it love to hear his passion for this place and the hotel. He started as a livery boy for his father's business bringing patrons up from the valley to this location long before all these buildings were here. Your observation about his love for the view was correct. He mentions that other Catskill hotels may be nice, but none have the magnificent view of the Catskill Mountain House Hotel. He often tells patrons the hotel is free; he only charges for the view. Anyway, I must attend to some business now," Liz said with a reservation in her voice, which encouraged me to believe she would rather have continued spending time together.

The office staff seemed relieved she had returned and soon Liz was surrounded by her staff and overwhelmed with queries. Sebastian, the hotel dog recognized me and wagged his tail. I started to walk away when I felt Liz gently take my arm from behind.

"I had a nice time with you today, Karl. I look forward to seeing you again, maybe later this evening," she said as I turned toward her and smiled.

"I would enjoy more time with you also, Liz," I said, before I continued down the hall toward the stairs leading up to my room.

Finally allowing myself to feel the ache in my bones and how tired I was, I struggled up the stairs to the third floor with my final burst of energy, removed my shoes and stretched out on the bed. Although earlier in the day I had considered a swim after my walk, that idea was quickly overruled. Certain that I would not sleep through dinner, I surmised the day had progressed well, and I fell asleep with an honest smile of contentment.

In what seemed like only a moment, I was awakened by the popping sounds of fireworks. It was darker now, but the sun had not set, and the sound of excited patrons and guests that came in waves through my hotel room window assured me I had not missed the fun. But I was sure I had missed dinner.

As I put on my shoes, I surmised the ten o'clock dimming of the lights would probably be postponed on this special evening. I had more important things to consider, such as where would I meet Liz tonight? Would it seem too forward to want to spend the evening, especially for the fireworks, with her by my side? Would Herr Strand be annoyed that she is "Collaborating inappropriately with the patrons," or whatever rules might be broken. More questions began to rattle in my mind.

I decided not to be bothered by the details and checked the evening's schedule leaflet, which had been slipped under my door during my rest. As the weather is unpredictable, especially for fireworks, I understood the need to disperse such plans to patrons at short notice. Based upon this brochure's exclamation, it seemed I had a plethora of choices.

Obviously designed to entice the interests of many different ages, the pamphlet offered, "The Catskill Mountain House is proud to invite patrons and friends of all ages to the most exciting place to be on this Independence Day! Fireworks, Music and more!" Here the leaflet listed all the evening's activities. "Ballroom Dancing featuring The Smiths Cornet Band" (get your dance card when you enter), "Music at the Pavilion by the Lake" featuring local talent,

"Light Games", "The best Fireworks Show in the Catskills" begins at 9:30 PM, and "Cobbler and ice cream on the portico after the fireworks, a hotel tradition. Hotel staff will be available for child observation. Tips appreciated."

This helped me to appreciate the reason Liz had to get back and coordinate her staff with the evening's festivities. I felt regretful that Liz most likely did not get to rest as I did.

Still wondering what "Light Games" meant, I walked down the stairs and out to the portico where many people were gathered and getting positioned for the fireworks show. Checking my pocket watch, I noticed it was not even 7:45 PM, and I decided my time could be better spent than squabbling over the best seat on the porch.

There were plenty of places to observe the fireworks, and I wanted to be with Liz. At that moment, I felt a slight tug of my arm as Liz came up behind me and asked me to follow her. Enthused that she was pleased to see me again and had found me first, I wondered where we were going.

"There's a band I want you to hear at the pavilion by the lake," she said as she took my hand when we reached the back of the hotel. This was the second time she took my hand; the first time was somewhat perfunctory due to the terrain and risk of slipping on the trails. This time, when she took my hand, the sparkle of light in her green eyes made me feel her true affection for me.

She then assured me that I was special. She stopped about halfway to the lake, turned to me, took both of my hands, and asked if she could be completely honest with me. I assured her it was the only way I conducted myself and offered as affirmation that, "The nuns in school affected me at a young age. They gave me a moral compass for life."

Liz began, choosing her words carefully,

"Men sometimes come to the hotel and think my girls are going to do whatever they demand. Drunk and rich, they, sometimes, think we will come up to their rooms and…" At this I interrupted her to save her any embarrassing details we both understood.

"I'm sorry to hear about such things, and I'm sure you have a conversation with your girls about how to handle such situations," I said, assuming she was leading into confiding an incident in which

I could possibly offer my help or advice. What she said next surprised me.

"Herr Strand told me how hearts have been broken here at the hotel, and he officially discourages his staff from getting too close to the patrons. I introduced you to Herr Strand because he knows me, and knows I have genuine fondness for you due to the obvious open affection I have shown toward you in front of him and the hotel staff today. I know we have only known each other for a few hours, but I think you are a very special man, Karl," she said as she gently squeezed my hands.

"I appreciate your honesty and have been attracted to you since we first met," she said as she looked into my eyes.

"Your natural calmness and kindness are very refreshing and different from my city life, friends, and experiences," I said to let her know I felt the same about her. Still holding hands and with eyes fixed on each other we kissed gently. I noticed her skin looked even more radiant up close as her soft lips met mine. A rush overcame me, and I realized that this affection we had was very real and wonderful.

We both smiled and held hands as we continued toward the lake, where we could hear music playing in the distance. A small group of people were gathered around a man who was standing on a box, shouting while he thumped his hand on what I surmised was a Bible. I could not understand what he was saying but I could tell whatever it was, he meant it.

Liz and I both understood the irony as a young couple startled the budding preacher by coming out of the darkening woods behind his makeshift podium. Her hair was tousled, and I doubted they were reading scripture under a tree together. Startled but determined, the Bible thumper continued his rant as some walked away.

We continued toward the lake past the boathouse, and I could now see the makeshift pavilion, not more than a basic bandstand, where the musicians were performing. Although they were a rather eclectic collection of young and old musicians, they played lively tunes and the young crowd responded with much dancing and clapping.

The band members' apparel was profoundly utilitarian, more befitting a barn dance than a hotel of such stature as the Catskill Mountain House. I remembered that the brochure noted they were local musicians, and they were playing to their audience. No one seemed bothered by their attire or the rustic stage and atmosphere; I believed the young crowd enjoyed the less-structured music and dance.

We joined in the festivities by dancing together near the stage. The sun had set, and the ink-black lake water behind the pavilion reflected the evening clouds and provided a tranquil backdrop to the festivities. As we danced, I noticed that all the musicians were smiling as they performed. In my accounting business I had discovered that my musician and artist clients were the happiest people with which I worked. They loved what they did and were paid well for their talents.

Liz was obviously having a good time, and I enjoyed watching the lights and shadows cross her glowing smile as we danced and held hands. This would be an evening I would long remember, for we were falling in love.

"Light Games" and Cobbler

We were all startled from our merriment by the abrupt sound of fireworks behind us. Following the crowd, most of us walked quickly toward the hotel. My sympathy went out to the band who were quickly replaced in priority by colorful explosives. Some people stayed for the music and dancing, and the band seemed not to be slighted by the sudden reduction in their audience.

As I turned back to look, I noticed Pol and his girlfriend, whom I had not noticed previously, stayed for the music. I remembered he said she didn't like fireworks. Rather than crowding through the hotel, Liz and I walked around the south side of the hotel and found a place to sit near the flagpole.

"Before it gets much louder, I want to tell you a little story," Liz said as we settled on the rock ledge. "Grandma, who you met earlier, had a conversation with me last year about dreams. I told her I had dreamt about one of my gardens; that I visited the garden in the winter and felt badly I could not plant yet. As usual, only parts of the dream made sense. Grandma told me about a similar dream she had."

"This dream repeated every year, soon after she would harvest her garden. She dreamt that she would check her garden at the end of the season, but then remember another garden she planted further up a hill behind a small grove of trees. Not one to ever forget a garden, she dreamt of walking to the other garden and noticed it had not been tended to. Although this was distressing to a gardener such as her, she was still able to gather some vegetables of use. I told her the garden represented the babies she lost, and that they were able to prosper in God's care and she need not worry. She took my hand, cried, and thanked me for my insight."

A loud boom shook us from our melancholy moment, as fireworks shot off from the ledge in front of the hotel. A man worked his way along the precipice holding a lighted signal flare, stooping along the way lighting off the fireworks. An impressive variety of colored streamers, exploding bursts and flares impressed the crowd; a baby could be heard crying in the few brief lulls of detonations, but otherwise they were silent in awe of this amazing spectacle.

Large, dark, moving shadows of the people flickered against the white front of the hotel. Surely echoes of our explosions were heard for miles and the lights from the fireworks must have been seen in the valley below. More fireworks were lit; it seemed the air could not hold more smoke. A large, rather putrid cloud of fireworks smoke found us at our location. Liz and I both coughed but decided not to lose our strategic location by leaving when the wind did not cooperate.

Knowing the expense of presenting such a spectacle made me appreciate why so many were celebrating here at our hotel. The hand pump fire engine I had observed by the lake was now near the front of the hotel, and two of the young firemen walked along the ledge looking carefully for any errant sparks in the woods below.

The fireworks continued until I could not calculate the cost anymore. Impressed and satiated, the crowd burst into applause as soon as we were sure it had ceased. Herr Strand emerged from his cliff perch, took a bow in front of the portico stairs, then tipped his hat and earned a rousing ovation.

Liz surprised me with a gentle kiss on my cheek. I was delighted by her show of affection, which she demonstrated all day. A quick look of pleasure, a squeeze of my hand, or a soft touch reassured me that this was genuine.

Herr Strand asked for our attention, and said it was, "Time for the Light Games to begin."

Still confused, I waited patiently as they dimmed the hotel lights, and a very bright spotlight on the roof of the Mountain House was electrified and pointed down the valley. Liz observed my puzzled expression and explained that ships on the Hudson will shine a light back when our light finds them on the river.

A slight breeze removed the residual smoke, and in a few minutes our spotlight met the light of a northbound ship in a curious exhibition of illumination courtship. As this only lasted a minute or two, without significant delay another ship moving southbound met our light. These "Light Games" continued for some time and the crowd's interest never waned.

Liz stood up promptly and said she must get to the kitchen to help with the cobbler dessert for everyone. Saying quick goodbyes, I admired her dedication to her work as I watched her slip through the crowd with purpose. Tired before the music, dance, and fireworks, I slowly walked toward the portico steps.

Children with small plates of apple cobbler and ice cream scurried down the steps. There were two lines of adults lining the main hall. One line was for the sweet course in the dining hall; the other line was queued to the bar. A man how-came-you-so who obviously missed the fireworks from his bar stool, stumbled by the lines in the hall as he gently bounced off the floral-patterned wall. I hoped he would find his room.

Having missed dinner, the cobbler dessert sounded quite good. Everyone let children move to the front of the line, which added to my continued appreciation for how polite people were at the hotel. I found a place to sit near Ol' Bill in the foyer, and promptly apologized for not introducing myself during our last conversation. I made sure he had received his dessert, and we discussed the war again like old friends. Finished with my sweets, I considered the possibility of spending more time with Liz that evening. But my tired body combined with an opportunity to celebrate a perfect day convinced me to go to my room without delay, and sleep. I said goodnight to Bill, and as I shuffled up the stairs to the second floor, I heard music coming from the ballroom. Curiosity overtook my exhaustion, and I walked down the hall leading to the ballroom doors.

"Need a dance card?" an attractive young woman asked me as I entered the spacious room. I thanked her for the card and approached some tables with chairs positioned where I could watch the band and the dancing. An elderly couple was sitting at the table, and I questioned if I could pass time with them. They nodded approvingly as I looked over to my right at the band.

The musicians were all similarly dressed in very neat matching striped shirts and black pants. "The Smiths Cornet Band" was well painted on a wooden sign placed at the front of the slightly raised bandstand where they performed. Long, white curtains flowed from the breezes coming through the French doors open behind the bandstand.

The music was perfunctory, but lively enough to keep my interest. I took a quick look at the dance card and realized there was only one dance I knew - "The Waltz". The women's long, elegant gowns swept the floor as their equally smartly appareled dance partners swung them about.

The participants were distinctly older than the partakers at the pavilion by the lake, and their perfunctory dance moves were rhythmic enough to almost lull me to sleep in my chair. Fully realizing my fatigue and having grasped that this ballroom was undoubtedly not going to become any more exhilarating, I decided to say goodnight to my elderly acquaintances and head up the final set of stairs to my room. A hotel bed had never felt so good.

In the morning dark I was awakened yet again by the bell and server's announcement of the eminent sunrise. I decided to enjoy my return to sleep after I considered my itinerary for the day and prioritized seeing the falls everyone talked about.

Having witnessed the fun spirit displayed the day before by passengers in the carriage by the two lakes, I was excited and determined to investigate such transportation. I knew Liz would have to work, but I did not know her schedule. To spend as much time as I could with Liz in the few remaining days of my visit at the Mountain House was my new objective. I prepared for the day, and as I adjusted my collar in the mirror, I remembered that the vanity was part of my tub, and a bath that evening would be pleasant.

Having missed dinner, the smell of bacon and coffee reached me as soon as I reached the top of the stairwell, further enticing my voracious mood. When I reached the first floor, I mingled with a small but talkative group as we walked into the dining hall.

Most patrons were seated at tables as other small groups filed into the dining hall. When the doors from the kitchen flew open and servers brought the steaming dishes to the tables, fewer gasps of surprise from the guests led me to believe that their comfort with this procedure was due to familiarity and some longevity to their visit here.

While I pondered in what manner the hotel determined how much staff to employ and food to prepare based upon the day of the week and (of course) the expenses entailed, I was asked by the gentleman to my left to pass the oatmeal. After obliging his request, I inquired as to his occupation.

"Bannerman's the name," he said proudly as he thrusted his hand in mine as if we just completed an important business transaction.

"I work in the surplus business," he continued. I told him the name sounded familiar, to which he replied, "I can tell by your accent you're from the city too. You may have seen my castle on your way up the Hudson." It is not common to meet someone who owns a castle, so I inquired further.

"After the Civil War, I purchased all the war surplus I could secure and opened a store in the heart of the city. The store and nearby storage included arms and explosive material that the city elders did not want in a crowded city for obvious reasons. I purchased an island and stored my surplus there. I had the castle built and live there now. It is beautiful with walkways and flower gardens," he said proudly.

Anticipating the question people must ask, he offered,

"My wife and I have been patrons of this beautiful hotel and location for years. I am friends with Herr Strand and have much respect for him and his accomplishments. Believe it, one can occasionally become tired of a castle."

That accomplished men respect other similar men did not surprise me. I surmised he provided the Civil War kepis to the children, and I inquired him of such.

"Why yes." He said looking pleased and surprised, I assumed and hoped, because he was impressed with my observation. Someone of his success and stature undoubtedly had accountants, but I expressed my profession nonetheless and gave him my card. He took it and read the address. "Your office is near Grand Central Terminal," he said, with the prided knowledge of New York shared by city residents. "I'll wager you'll be glad when they finish it," he continued.

"The construction is especially unpassable on 42nd street, and most days Lexington is the same," I concurred, hoping he would express interest in my services. We proceeded to enjoy our hot cakes and syrup, coffee, and oatmeal. I did not want to disturb our breakfast, but I hoped he would continue to tell me more about his business and the castle. "Did you enjoy the fireworks last evening?"

I asked, as I labored to think of a way to continue our conversation while I passed a bowl of fruit.

"I did," Mr. Bannerman replied. "But my wife doesn't like all the noise. We danced a while and went to bed early," he said with a contented smile. I wondered how long he had been married, and he had the pleasant calmness of a man who was pleased with his position in life.

I wondered if we would have another opportunity to discuss his business experience and how he became successful.

"I think I've had enough to eat this morning," he said as he patted his belly and gave me a wink. "With a name like Debacher I bet you like beer. Maybe we can have a beer later at the bar," he offered. I accepted his offer, and we said goodbye.

The Falls

Laurel House and Kaaterskill Falls

I walked down the hall and once again enjoyed the smell of the pine boughs that ringed posts and balusters. Looking for Liz in the office, I saw Sebastian, the dog, chewing on a bone bigger than him.

"Madelyn, correct?" I said to the young woman in the office who was typing at the oak check-in desk.

"Yes," she said excitedly, as she seemed to appreciate that I remembered her name. She removed the typed template from the typewriter and placed it on a mimeograph machine on a nearby table in the office.

"How's Sebastian doing with that bone?" I asked.

"He is spoiled. People feel sorry for his bad leg and give him treats. He loves chicken, and Chef Kris often saves some just for him. Some people don't like no dogs, so we try to keep him in the office most of the time," Madelyn said as she looked lovingly at the little dog.

"Who takes care of him when the hotel is closed?" I asked out of concern for the little canine.

"Oh, he's my dog. I brought him in one day because he wasn't feeling well, and I didn't want to leave him alone. Herr Strand heard him bark and I thought I would lose my job! I was pleasantly surprised when Herr Strand picked him up and asked about his leg. Sebastian licked Herr Strand's face and, thankfully, he laughed and called Sebastian, *'Der kleiner hund,'* ('The little dog,'), Madelyn said, happy to convey what turned out to be acceptable to the hotel owner. "Herr Strand said Sebastian could stay in my office and if he heard any patron complaints about the dog, he would let me know." Anticipating my query, Madelyn stated, "Liz is watering flowers. I'm sure you could see her if you step out the back door."

I thanked her and walked out the back away from the long morning shadow of the hotel. Where the hotel shadow ended and the sunlight began, I saw Liz's broad-brimmed sun bonnet and the warm breeze ruffling her dress softly. I called to her, and as she raised her head, she peeked past her hat brim and smiled at me. She continued in her work, emptying buckets of water placed on the back of a simple pull cart. As I approached her, I noticed a few goats tethered by rope eating the grass near the circular drive and stone pylons.

"They love the grass, and it frees up the men to do other chores than cut the lawn," Liz said as I walked close to her. "I must be sure the rope keeps them away from paths and hotel patrons. One woman said the goats looked mean. I never understood that. One time a goat ate some paint the men left on the ground. There was food nearby, but the goat ate the paint. Didn't do it any harm," Liz said as she poured water on the flowers.

"I'll finish up here and we can sit by the beach if you'd like," she said as she dragged the cart to another row of flowers. Not wanting to distract her from her work, I told Liz I would wait at the nearby beach.

The sun seemed hotter with every minute as I walked past the circular drive and service barns and followed signs to North Lake Beach. I secured a chair tucked in the shade trees behind the boathouse, and watched children splash each other while I also kept an eye out for Liz. Another beautiful, warm sunny day in the mountains with the clouds reflected on the lake helped me into a relaxed mood.

A small "toot!" of a train horn came from the Otis Summit Station behind me. I wondered if that meant a train would pass by soon? A soft touch on my shoulder somewhat startled me as I was pleasantly surprised to see it was Liz.

"Beautiful here, isn't it?" Liz said as she sat down in a chair next to me. I inquired if she must return to her duties. "After working late last night, this morning I asked Herr Strand if I could take leisure this afternoon and work this evening instead. He told me he trusted me, liked my dedication, and that he understood. He called it, 'Menschlike Nature,' or something similar. But he agreed to give me the afternoon so I can spend it with you," she said excitedly, which continued to assure me of her sincerity and honest affection.

"I must return to work. I will be available after lunch is served," she said, and we briefly touched hands as she rose from her chair.

"Would it be possible to take a carriage to the falls today?" I asked as she started to walk away. She turned toward me and said, "There is a list in the office for carriage ride requests. Usually there is enough interest that carriages run a few times a day back and forth to the Overlook Mountain House, the Hotel Kaaterskill, and the Laurel House. I'll add our names when I get back to the hotel."

She smiled and we agreed to meet after lunch near the office. I was pleased to ponder that a fun carriage ride to see the falls would be an advantageous opportunity to get to know each other better and further develop our mutual affection.

I considered a brief dip into the lake as I had some time before lunch. Comfortable in my chair, out of the sun, beautiful view, relaxed and content in my day plans convinced me I did not need to go anywhere. I watched as children swam with their parents and siblings. A train started out of Otis Summit Station and then headed between the lakes into the woods on the other side of the lakes. I watched until I could no longer follow the smoke trail through the trees in the distance.

A soft, cool breeze off the lake met me in the shade trees and smelled like pine. I closed my eyes and felt calmer than I had in quite a while. I was startled by the loud clanging of oars placed in a boat as a couple prepared to row around the lake. They briefly smiled at me as they dragged the boat into the water, then he helped her into the vessel. As they both appreciated the simple pleasure of rowing leisurely around a small lake in the mountains, I realized that my priorities were becoming readjusted.

The sophisticated life I led in the city was beginning to pale by comparison to the effortless beauty of uncomplicated living. The pace of life in New York City was consistently increasing in intensity. The extremely competitive nature of the city seemed to exaggerate a false feeling of limited resources. I felt none of that here.

Maybe, as I looked around, the vastness of the mountains and wilderness lead to an openness of sharing because resources seemed almost limitless. A lack of competitiveness seemed to also portend a more considerate atmosphere. Several times hotel patrons had asked how I was and listened to my response instead of a perfunctory retort.

The prospect of another rewarding meal before our excursion finally caused me to pry from my chair. As I walked toward the hotel, I noticed the goats had been moved to a new location, content in their grazing as before. A carriage pulled up to the pylons on the circular drive and kicked up some dust as it stopped. Interested in the variety of travelers who might depart, I wondered if there were any goat haters among them. I decided my hunger had priority and continued toward the hotel.

Little shade was afforded by the noon overhead sun, and a few slender worker men with white shirts, grey coveralls and long black beards were enjoying a smoke in the only shade afforded them near the back entrance of the hotel. I nodded to them as I entered the hotel and waited for my eyes to adjust to the reduced light.

Madelyn had Sebastian on a short rope and was leading him out the door as we passed each other in the hall. I noticed Sebastian did not rest much on his crippled leg but used it to pivot and steady himself as he leaned and walked on the other three legs. I said hello to Madelyn and turned to see one of the worker men bend down and pet Sebastian as they stepped outside. I continued up the stairs to my room to wash up before lunch and went straight to the dining room for another rewarding meal.

I saw Mr. Bannerman at another table, and it appeared he was pressing the flesh like a politician and touting his accomplishments as before. I attempted to engage in meaningful conversation with the fellow patrons at my table to no avail, except a serious-looking gentleman to my right. He introduced himself as Dr. Flaacke, a veterinarian from Albany. I introduced myself and we exchanged business cards.

When I inquired about his specialty, he answered, "Horses. But I treat a few cows when requested." His face seemed to soften a little as he described his work. "Most days I just patch scrapes on horses. Poultices and such. I service and travel to livery stables, carriage houses and farms in the rolling hills of the Albany area. Troy is impossible in the winter as the streets are so steep," the doctor said, much to my pleasure as I reveled in such occupation detail. With honest interest I asked for the oddest animal he had treated in his profession.

"Well...when the Barnum and Bailey Circus came through, they requested help from local veterinarians. I answered the call and helped patch an elephant's leg. But the monkey was the strangest. As I attended the simian's small cut, he stroked my hair and gently touched my arm as if he understood I was there to help. I think monkeys are smarter than we believe."

Unexpectedly, my potentially dull lunch had become an interesting foray into a profession in which I had no experience. I finished my tongue-and-Swiss sandwich, and as we said our farewell, I thanked the doctor for our conversation and walked down the hall toward the front portico. I suppressed my displeasure at having not discovered the salary of a veterinarian.

The noon-day sun was keeping the patrons captive under the colorful sunshades provided on the tables near the front of the hotel. As I reached the bottom of the porch steps the hustle of servers bringing cool drinks with ice from the bar, couples walking, children running and playing, and the general activity of the hotel made me ponder how lifeless this white behemoth building must seem when there are no patrons, no workers...nobody.

I returned from my melancholy daydream to notice the elderly couple I met with Liz were enjoying iced tea and reading to children sitting on the grass listening attentively to "Grandma". Returning to the hotel office I asked Madelyn when the next carriage to the Laurel House was scheduled. Assured we would be leaving within the hour, I decided to take a short walk to the blacksmith shop I had observed on a map of the area in the dining hall.

As I walked north along the path near the front of the hotel, I passed a separate white three-story building with a connecting hallway to the hotel. A sign indicated this was where hotel employees resided. I had never been so forward as to ask Liz about her living arrangements at the hotel, but I assumed this was her summer accommodations.

The blacksmith shop was past the employee housing just before the ground sloped down into the woods. It was a simple three-wall wooden structure with large stall doors open in the front. The shop had thick walls and belched smoke out of a hefty brick chimney. Looking inside I could see buckets, horseshoes, and many tools of the blacksmith trade hanging on the dark walls all around the inside of the structure. There was just enough room for a two-horse stall in the left-hand side of the building.

Not wanting to disturb their work I stepped quietly out of the sun into the sooty, smoky dark entrance of the workshop. Tripping on a brick as I entered drew the attention of a man beating a horseshoe on an anvil near the roaring, unbearably hot fire in a brick oven. He was a hefty, black-bearded man wearing long leather gloves and a thick black overall. I apologized for my intrusion, but he was very cordial and invited me into the shop.

He continued to bang the red-hot horseshoe as another man with a full, white beard gently consoled a horse in one of the stalls. I noticed him stroke the horse and speak to the animal in kind tones. He seemed to fumble and have trouble as he reached for a brush on a stool near the horse. The burly blacksmith noticed my concern as he pumped bellows to stoke the fire.

"Victor's my name. That's old Hank with the horse. He may be blind, but he is a big help with all the animals here, especially the horses. Has a kind, gentle way about him that keeps the horses calm with all the banging and shoeing. He can identify the color of any horse by touching it," shouted the muscular blacksmith without stopping the loud, ringing battering on the anvil.

Certain my head would hurt all day if I stayed much longer, my suspicion that this was not a popular attraction for the hotel patrons was affirmed when Victor said, "We don't get many visits at this shop from the people staying at the hotel. If you have any questions let me know." I noticed a small, metal stand with a bowl-like structure on top and asked how it was used. "That's my knife maker. I make custom knives. Herr Strand loved the one I made for him. I have some knife blanks started and can shape, finish, sharpen and add a handle in a day if you would like one," Victor said proudly in a husky voice earned inhaling smoke all day.

"I would be pleased to have a hand-made knife from you," I said as I was sure it would make an interesting conversation piece with friends back in the city. We agreed on a price for a "Bowie" style knife with a bone handle. I offered to pay now but he was fine with me paying the next day. I thanked him for his time and said goodbye to Hank who waved to me over his shoulder while he brushed a horse.

I returned to the hotel and passed a group of children being led by two of Liz's girls. The children were excited for their play adventure, and their smiling faces and giggles made me appreciate what a lively hotel this was. All ages appeared to find reasons for contentment here. Familiarity with the hotel continued as I began to sadly contemplate my departure in a couple of days. Would Liz ever visit me in New York? Would this be a relationship we could continue to nurture with letters and infrequent visits? Would she find the city as interesting and exotic as I do the mountains?

As I walked down the hall and appreciated the pine bough smells once more, I noticed Liz come in the back door and walk in the office. She was carrying a basket with flowers and was easily recognizable even from a distance due to her large sun hat. I entered the office as Liz was placing the flowers in vases from a shelf. She smiled as I entered the room. Sebastian left the comfort of his office bed to smell my shoes, and he wagged his tail as I gently scratched his back.

"I have a few chores I must attend to before we leave for the Laurel House. Don't forget to bring some coins for the falls. I also would like you to meet a friend of mine out in the barns," she said as she placed the flowers gently in each vase. "We can walk out there and then meet the carriage in the circular drive around one o'clock. Does that sound OK?" she asked as Madeline checked in new hotel guests beside us. I checked my pocket watch and we agreed to meet in the back of the hotel in ten minutes. I took the opportunity to walk to my room and wash up before our trip.

As I walked up the stairs, I noticed the bright sunlight that came down through the glass at the top of the staircase. Just as each wing of the hotel surrounded a courtyard that allowed more sunlight into the rooms, I appreciated that this structural design element incorporated natural light that offered the spiral staircase and the middle of the hotel an open presence. I was reminded that Grand Central Station in the city also has large windows; otherwise, the Grand Concourse would be an exceptionally large, dark room.

I reached my room and as I turned the white porcelain handle, a card wedged in the door fell onto the floor. It was an invitation to the "Best Wednesday Night Ballroom Dance in Town, 8:00 PM, Formal attire required." I smiled at the creative nature of the hotel notices and wondered if Madelyn was responsible.

I poured water into my wash basin and freshened my face and hands. When I grabbed the towel hanging off the vanity, I reminded myself to take a well-deserved bath this evening, especially after another dusty carriage ride. As I removed the towel from my face, I noticed coins on my dresser top which reminded me that Liz asked me to bring them. I swept the Liberty Head V Nickels and Indian Head pennies into my pocket, put on my boots, and left for the stairs.

My shadow was before me on the steps, as I continued to enjoy the sunlight from the dome ring of glass panes at the peak of the staircase. As I reached the bottom of the stairs and walked down the hall toward the back of the hotel, I hoped Herr Strand did not change his mind, or Liz was needed for the afternoon.

I stepped out into the afternoon sun I was pleasantly surprised to see her waiting at a table under a tree. She had her customary sun hat and wore a brightly colored flower-covered dress. The large rim of her sun hat shielded me from her view until I was almost next to her. She turned slowly and smiled as she recognized me.

I returned the smile and held out my hand. She placed her hand in mine and we walked toward the circular drive without saying a word for a long moment. A large, very rugged-looking man in a tan jacket walked by us.

"Hello, Stu," she said as he tipped his hat to us. When he had passed us, she added, "His name is Kurt. He hunts this land all year and is very helpful as he snares the annoying rabbits. We call him Stu because he makes good rabbit stew. The jacket he wears is buckskin."

"So that is from a deer he killed?" I asked, unfamiliar with any hunting practices.

"Yes. He wastes nothing of what he takes. He makes his own clothes from deerskin, and rabbit fur lines his boots in the winter," she said while I tried my best to understand how people so close to New York City could possibly live so differently.

She let go of my hand and hugged my arm as we both tried to talk.

"I'm glad you were able to spend the afternoon with me today," I said. Liz said at the same moment, "I think you'll love the falls." I repeated my pleasure of having her company for the day. We continued to walk in and out of the sparse shade provided by the few trees between the hotel and several barns and stables near the circular drive. She explained that the pylons on the circular drive lined up with the rear hotel entrance, so that if there were a fog people could simply walk straight into the hotel.

I asked her about the ballroom dance the next evening and she seemed quiet for a moment and somewhat pensive. I then realized my ignorance and asked her if she would accompany me to the dance. She startled me with her excited positive response.

"Of course, I would be pleased to accompany you to the ball tomorrow. Oh, here we are at the barns where I want you to meet Jackie," she said as she hugged my arm and opened the wooden, noticeably hand-whittled barn door handle.

Adjusting to the sudden diminished light, I struggled to see my surroundings. My nose, however, was quick to recognize the scent of pine so familiar in the hotel. I had a strange feeling of being one of the few patrons to view the usually private intricate interplay of so many people needed to keep such a hotel operating. Piles of pine branches were against one wall of the barn, and a few finished pine boughs so abundant in the hotel were lying nearby.

Hay bales, farm tools and a horse cart filled the few remaining spaces in the small barn. A large, older black woman was sitting in a rocking chair near one of the two windows in this otherwise drearily dark building. She appeared to be knitting or sewing, slowly rocking to her own gentle singing.

"So good to see you child," she said with a heavy southern accent as we approached her. "Who's your fine-looking friend?" she said, as I took her hand and introduced myself. Again, as with Liz's friend Eliza, she seemed surprised at my cordiality toward her.

"Jackie does all our sewing. She made matching dresses for my girls, repairs curtains and makes the pine boughs too," Liz said as the two smiled at each other with obvious shared affection.

"You ain't plannin' on staying all day in this musty barn with hay and 'ol me. What plans 'ya have for this beautiful day?" Jackie asked.

"We're going to the falls. Herr Strand has been very kind to give me time to spend with Mr. Debacher," Liz said. Jackie offered,

"Well child, ain't none of the girls seen you happier than lately. You must be something special, Mr. Debacher," Jackie said, causing me to blush. However, it felt wonderful to get continued affirmation of her honest affection.

Not wanting the awkward moment to linger any longer, Liz said, "Mr. Debacher has invited me to the Ballroom Dance tomorrow night. I am excited, as I have watched but never participated except to serve and clean. How wonderful to be part of such a formal event, twirling in my dress to dance to music! I will have to work on finding a dress when we get back from the falls," Liz said excitedly. I realized how important this event would be to her and felt poorly that I was not initially more sensitive to the subject. She must have fretted about whether I would invite her.

"Well, you have a nice time together at the falls. Say hello to our friends at the Laurel House. So nice to meet you Mr. Debacher," Jackie said as we headed toward the door and back into the sunlight.

We walked by the cow barns, chicken coops, and vegetable gardens surrounded by low fences. An obvious reason for the enclosures, a rabbit ran quickly out of sight near one of the gardens.

"We have to check the fences constantly," said Liz. "One small opening and the rabbits can destroy a garden in an evening," she continued. "Yesterday a hawk took out one of our chickens. No one saw it happen, but we know it was a hawk," she said with such conviction I inquired further.

"How do you know what took the chicken?" I asked, as I assumed there were several opportunistic animals who might enjoy such a bird.

"Well, when a fox takes a chicken, the ground is torn up and a trail of feathers and blood in the grass is a sure sign of the struggle. When a hawk takes a chicken, there are a couple of feathers and not much else left behind," Liz said, as she continued to amaze me with her knowledge of the natural order of her environment.

We waited at a table under a tree for the carriage to the Laurel House to arrive. I asked if we needed tickets, but Liz said we were fine.

"I have seen Thomas Cole paintings in the city depicting the falls. They look remarkable," I said as the carriage arrived at the circular drive. We held hands and boarded the large carriage which seated at least a dozen occupants. The carriage resembled a large wagon with seats facing front and a foot rail along the side which allowed one to step up into each row of seats.

It was covered with a wooden frame over which stretched a heavy, green material, with white fringes. Hanging colored streamers gave the vehicle a whimsical appearance. The driver, who sat in a single seat, gave out a loud "Heya!" as the four horses needed to pull the cart jerked forward and pressed us back into our seats.

We passed the beach, boat house and music pavilion and paralleled the railroad tracks sharing the narrow passage between the lakes. Another "Heya!" from our driver as the horses dug into the dirt to get us up the incline past the lakes.

As we twisted up a narrow road through the woods, Liz reached into a bag under our seat and handed me a small, toy horn to blow as we passed another carriage near the top of the ridge. I looked around the carriage and realized we had quite a varied collection of young and old passengers.

A glint of sunlight caught a silver flask as it was handed back and forth between riders in the back of the wagon. We blew horns, yelled hello, and waved furiously to other passing travelers which was unquestionably fun for us all. I truly enjoyed our time together, and she never stopped smiling from the moment we left the circular drive. I leaned in for a quick kiss, and she obliged my advance.

"It is a short ride to the Laurel House. I have several friends who work there. I have tried to get them work at the Mountain House. Herr Strand pays better than Mr. Schutt," Liz said as the carriage settled into a leisurely pace on a flat expanse of road.

Liz handed me a large bell.

"A cow bell," she said, looking somewhat incredulous that I was unfamiliar with the instrument. I rang the bell just as a slightly dour-looking woman behind me blew a horn and could not hide her subsequent smile of satisfaction.

Our carriage took a sharp left as we headed past signs guiding us toward a well-maintained road and the direction of the Laurel House and falls. Within moments we arrived at a circular drive in front of the hotel and stopped to disembark. I stepped off first and offered my hand to Liz to help her down the small steps near our driver. I thanked him for his service and tipped him as is customary in the city.

He expressed gratitude and said, "I recommend taking the stairs to the falls and then having a rum punch in the log cabin. I'll be coming by this hotel from Overlook around 4:00 PM." I looked at my watch and surmised we had a few hours to explore the surroundings. Liz grabbed my arm and said,

"The falls will be there. I want you to meet a friend at the hotel."

The Laurel House was much smaller than the Catskill Mountain House and certainly not many hotels could rival the sheer bulk of the Hotel Kaaterskill. Thirteen three-story, square pillars defined the front of the hotel and the center stairs led to a long front portico similar to the other hotels. A light-yellow exterior with white trim led up to a red roof finished by a flag waving on a cupola at the center of the roofline.

The upper floor rooms each had individual balconies protruding from the hotel facade. As we entered the hotel and lobby area, I did not feel confined by the smaller space but rather I felt a warm environment that pleased my senses. To our left a large, green-colored desk with the open hotel ledger book on the counter wrapped around the smiling front desk attendant. Green wallpaper trim and pale blue walls defined the lobby area that led to a set of stairs in front of us.

"Can you tell me where Marian is?" Liz inquired of the friendly desk attendant.

"She's cleaning upstairs. Do you want me to ring her?" he asked.

"Oh no. Please let her know Liz is here when you see her," Liz said with a smile. He let her know he would relay the message as she grabbed my arm to leave the lobby. I asked Liz if we could look around the hotel and she obliged.

The Kaaterskill Clove

Following signs to the ballroom we observed an empty room except for a piano in the far corner. The window frames and trim continued the green colors we observed in the lobby. The high ceiling was divided by wallpaper into large geometric shapes, and several floor-to-ceiling windows lined the wall facing the front of the hotel.

The middle of the front wall had a small fireplace with a perfectly angled mirror above for self-admiration during ballroom activities, I assumed. We returned to the lobby and followed signs toward the dining area. Pink colored tablecloths covered about twenty-five small tables with a stage at the end of the room.

Well-polished wooden floors and gold-colored curtains filtered the hot afternoon sun into the room. Not as fancy as the Hotel Kaaterskill dining arrangement, but not as simple as the Catskill Mountain House dining hall.

"The Laurel House is less expensive than the other hotels," Liz said quietly, I assumed so as not to sound judgmental and possibly be heard by any nearby patrons or staff. As we left the hotel, I mentioned I met a young couple on the steamship who were staying at the Laurel House. Liz noted that it was a popular honeymoon destination.

"The cozy atmosphere of a smaller hotel, the falls, nearby walking trails and the ability to easily visit other hotels make this a popular hotel," Liz said as we walked down the front steps off the porch. "But I believe the Laurel House is mostly popular because it is almost one half the cost of the other hotels," she said as we were outside and had little risk of offending anyone with her comments.

I could hear the rush of a river as we walked down a pathway angled from the front of the hotel toward the falls. We passed couples who nodded graciously as we passed a few trees near the circular drive and our pathway. A wooden fence to our left kept patrons from slipping on the glistening wet rocks in the flowing river that was rushing toward the falls.

The mist from the falls momentarily obstructed our view, and we stopped behind the wooden fence by the log cabin which was perched on the edge of the precipice. Signs on the cabin invited us in for refreshments and "Quench Your Thirst by the Falls".

A man who stood behind a small bar to our left, gave us a pleasant nod; a few tables and chairs were scattered to our right. I followed Liz's lead as we walked to the back of the building and stepped onto a deck worryingly perched on the same ridge as the falls to our left.

The mist temporarily lifted toward the sky revealing the true grandeur of the view down the valley. Beautiful green and blue-green folds of mountains overlapping each other from the left and the right far into the distance. Each fold was a different hue of natural splendor, lighter shades of blue-green lost in the mist of the distant hills. Truly a great place for a hotel, I thought. I noticed a long pole with a rope on the end tied to a bucket hanging from the deck rail.

"We need to pay Mr. Schutt to open the falls," Liz said. I gave her a confused look which was now familiar to her. "If we pay a quarter dollar to Mr. Schutt, he takes some boards off the stream and releases the water over the falls," she said, in a manner that led me to believe this had been a common practice here at the Laurel House for many seasons.

View from top of Kaaterskill Falls

"I remembered to bring some coins as you asked," I said as we turned to walk out the cabin and back along the fence by the river. We stopped by a small dam by a bridge that was effectively reducing the flow. A skinny older man with a long white beard similar in appearance and age to Herr Strand came down the walkway from the hotel with a few people trying to get his attention in conversation. He seemed to be uninterested in their banter as he made a determined turn toward our direction and offered a big smile to us both.

"Schutt's the name. Pleased to meet you and welcome to the Laurel House. Quarter a piece and I'll open the falls for you. You're a friend of Marian's who works for the Catskill Mountain House, yes?" He said to Liz in a calm manner as he shook my hand. Liz acknowledged his query with a positive nod as I pulled out coins in my pocket, picked out two Liberty Head Quarters and handed them to Mr. Schutt.

He was quick to ask the other patrons for the same. When satisfied that anyone within eyesight had paid for the privilege, he removed the boards as Liz excitedly grabbed my arm and led me across a small bridge crossing the river by the dam. We followed a path on the other side back toward the falls and began a long descent down a set of quite intimidating stairs.

We unlocked our arms and grabbed the slippery, moist rails wet from the mist of the falls near us. The stairs were an impressive structure, with small landings from which to observe the changing view of the valley below. I mentioned to Liz I was impressed with the stairs.

"Marian said it is three hundred steps and almost one hundred feet down," Liz said as I continued to marvel at the structure as well as the magnificent view. One of the landings crossed behind the falls itself. We stopped and I hugged her closely. She smiled at me, and no words were necessary. Her beauty, the falls, and the valley view all contributed to a wonderful moment.

We continued down the stairs at the other side of the falls and stepped onto a large, flat rock. As we walked along a rock ledge that curved behind the falls, water cascaded over the precipice above us into a rocky, bowl-like pool below.

"People have been hurt trying to walk down to the pool," Liz said, and I noticed it did look quite dangerous to attempt. We shuffled carefully along the rocky outcrop as the sound of the falls were amplified by the natural amphitheater. Directly behind the falling cascade under a protruding ledge was the entrance to a small cave.

"Is it dangerous to enter a cave here?" I asked with the trepidation of one who now was aware of bears in the area.

"I don't believe any bears are hibernating now," Liz said with a slight tease in her manner, aware of my earlier apprehension. We entered the cave and immediately I noticed the smell of wet dirt; the type of earthy smell you remember when as a child you fell in the mud or became very dirty. I took Liz's hand as we entered and walked slowly in as far as the light from the entrance allowed.

Green moss and lichen clung to the walls of the cave and had a strange texture I noted while I steadied myself with my other hand on the wall. The damp air became cooler as we further entered the cave. Soon we could only feel our steps and began to stumble in the darkness. I thanked Liz for the opportunity to become a cave explorer. She smiled at me and could tell I was having a wonderful time with her and these experiences. We turned and walked back toward the entrance.

The cool air was soon replaced by the much warmer, humid air of summer. I was surprised to notice the aroma of plants as we reentered the sunny day. In a short time, the cave, being void of any such life, made me appreciate the abundance of living things and wonderful colors the world of darkness we just visited never had. We walked back toward the bottom of the stairs and walked up to the first landing.

The bucket I had seen earlier at the log cabin at the top of the falls was on the end a rope dangling in reach of us on the landing. Liz grabbed the bucket and asked me for some coins. I handed her two Liberty Head Quarters. She scribbled something on a piece of paper, then placed the paper, pencil and coins in the bucket and gave the attached rope a couple of firm pulls. Soon the bucket was retrieved and returned in moments with two dishes of ice cream.

We enjoyed our cherry vanilla ice cream as the mist from the falls gently cooled us in the summer sun. The view continued in all its amazing splendor, infrequently veiled by the mist of the falls and a brief rainbow when the breeze blew toward the valley below. We kissed to seal a perfect moment and continued up the stairs, behind the falls to the top and back over the bridge in the direction of the hotel. Boards were placed back on the dam waiting for the next group of paying participants. As we walked by the circular drive and up a small incline near the hotel entrance, we were greeted by Liz's friend leaving the hotel.

"Marian, I want you to meet Mr. Debacher," Liz said after they had hugged and greeted each other. I took Marian's hand and noticed it was rough from the tough work she performed. Her face was perfect; she had a wonderful dark complexion. I wondered if she was of African origin or from another continent.

View from bottom of Kaaterskill Falls

Her accent had a slight lilt to it that was unfamiliar to me, as I had heard every type of accent at one time or another in New York City.

Liz and Marian continued in small talk as we all walked together toward the log cabin. We sat together and ordered the rum punches that came recommended by our wagon driver. "Oh, Jamaica makes the best rum in the world," Marian said, and then I identified her accent.

"Do you get back to Jamaica very often?" I asked.

"Oh no, we came here because my family wanted a better life. Every few year storms ravage our island country, and we must rebuild everything. My father lived through two such storms and was tired of it all. Besides, I would never have met my wonderful friend Liz if we still lived in Jamaica," Marian said as she hugged Liz. The cabin attendant brought us our drinks, then handed us a folder which contained pictures of the falls and hotel for purchase. I perused the photographs as we enjoyed our beverages.

"Let's take Mr. Debacher to the top of the hotel. The view down the valley is even better there," said Marian to Liz as Marian gently touched my arm.

"Could I see one of the rooms? I did not get to visit a room at the Kaaterskill Hotel, and my curiosity is irrepressible," I asked Marian.

"Of course. I will show our suite. It is where President Arthur stayed," Marian said with obvious pride.

"President Arthur visited here. That must have caused a stir," I offered as we finished our drinks. I returned the photos and tipped the cabin attendant, after which the three of us enjoyed a passing look at the falls and valley below from the cabin's precipitous rear deck. We left the quaint log cabin and passed other happy couples and patrons on the path back toward the hotel.

As we walked up the portico steps and entered the hotel, I noticed a sign posted near the front desk that noted, "The famous Germania Band from Philadelphia will be playing in the Ballroom this weekend." I was reminded that I would be in New York City by the weekend, without my lovely Liz by my side.

Attempting to avoid any more such despondent thoughts, we walked up the stairs near the front desk and Marian drew me back into the present with a loud, "Here it is!" as we reached the third floor. She opened a door with a plaque that read, "Chester A. Arthur Suite", with a key on a large ring with many other keys. I asked if we could enter the room and Marian nodded in approval.

Eager to compare the difference with my room at the Catskill Mountain House, I entered and looked around to familiarize myself with the furniture and adornments. Fine upholstered chairs, settees and rugs were all color matched to perfection. The suite was several times larger than my room, and I reminded myself this was designed for a President or other distinguished patron. A balcony afforded a great view from the front of the hotel.

As I stepped on the balcony, I envisioned the crowds that cheered the President as he waved his hat to the multitude of enthusiasts below. Marian indicated it was time to leave and I immediately obliged as I thanked her for the opportunity to experience such luxury at this hotel. We followed Marian who opened another locked door in the middle of the hall labeled "Observatory - ask for access at the front desk" to reveal a narrow staircase.

We followed Marian to the top of the hotel peak where a platform on which to stand allowed us to appreciate the perfect view afforded by the height. We could hear the falls below, and the mist rising from the precipice did not obscure the vastness of the valleys in the distance. Large, round cloud shadows that appeared at first to be patches of darker trees, moved slowly up the remote mountainous wilderness. Forested mountains folded over more mountains as my appreciation increased significantly for the beauty our nation offered before us. I continued to feast on the view as Marian and Liz participated in light conversation about their work.

"Sometimes at night Mr. Schutt has staff light rafts of burning wood and lets them float off the falls," Marian told us. Liz let Marian know I was taking her to the dance the following evening at the Catskill Mountain House. "I'll be workin' tomorrow night, but I sure would love to see you two dance together at the ball," Marian said, which encouraged me to believe she thought we made an attractive couple.

"That's very kind of you, Marian. I wish you could be there also," I said with the sincerity she hopefully perceived. The loud clopping of horses and the sound and view of a carriage in the circular drive reminded me to check my watch for the time.

"Our driver said he would be back from the Overlook Hotel around 4:00 PM. It is 3:20 PM. Would it be OK to play the piano in the ballroom? I was classically trained and respect the instrument," I requested of Marian.

I quickly realized that Marian was probably not of authority to make such a decision about hotel property. As I was about to apologize for my mistake Marian said, "I will check with the front desk attendant. We just don't like children pounding on the keys. Fine musicians play from time to time and the patrons love small concerts. I'm sure it would be OK."

We left the observation area and followed Marian to the first floor. Not that I would be so forward as to ask Marian another favor, but the request and possible excitement of seeing another room at the hotel was diminished by the thought of comparing the room with the "Chester A. Arthur Suite". Or my own room at the Catskill Mountain House, certainly.

After a brief exchange between Marian and the front desk clerk, I was given permission to play, and Marian led us to the ballroom where the piano I had noticed earlier sat alone in the empty room. Marian sensed our desire to be alone, and politely said she had some things to finish at the hotel.

I thanked her for her time and hospitality, and said I hoped to see her again. Liz said her goodbye and we sat together at the piano bench as I played some light tunes which echoed to every corner of the empty space. She rested her head on my shoulders as a small breeze came through the windows.

The soft voices of people outside could be heard coming from the front of the hotel, mixed with the faint sound of the falls in the distance. I played quietly, hoping to not attract an audience and disturb our private moment together.

"You play beautifully. Why didn't you tell me you were such a good musician?" Liz asked as she very gently stroked my back.

"My family forced me to learn at a young age. At first, of course, I hated the piano and practicing. I wanted to play in the street with my friends. As I grew older, I began to appreciate the ability to entertain myself and others. Now playing feels like a natural extension of my hands and mind, as I have been playing for so many years," I said, with confidence I had earned. "Do you know the piece I just played?" I asked, as I assumed she would know the popular song.

"I do not. What is it?" she inquired.

"It is 'After the Ball' and is the most popular song this year," I said, as I wondered why she would not know the tune.

"Everything comes late to upstate New York, especially the mountain towns," Liz said. I continued to play as the breeze moved the curtains in and out in successive rhythm down the wall of windows. I felt in harmony with my environment; the movement of the curtains, the music and Liz by my side felt perfect. Never did I imagine such a delightful vacation. I stopped to check my watch and mentioned the 4:00 PM departure time I was given by the carriage driver.

"Oh, they're never exactly on time. We call it 'Mountain Time', but there are many reasons why it is difficult for carriages to be on time here. Weather, rattlesnakes, deer, broken wheels…the roads are well maintained, and the drivers do their best. But the only things around here on time are the meals and the trains," Liz said with the confidence of her years of experience. I finished playing and we hugged at the piano for a moment.

"Let's go out front and wait for our carriage," I said, continuing in my belief that the carriage would be on time. Liz obliged and we sat at a table in the shade near the hotel entrance, in full view of the circular drive. I asked Liz if I could get her something to drink in the log cabin. As she was about to respond, our carriage pulled into the drive from our right and turned in front of the hotel. I helped her into the carriage and reached for a cow bell under our seat. Liz found a horn and together we produced a cacophony for our exit from the Laurel House property.

Our carriage returned to the end of the road and took a right toward the lakes and Mountain House. We took another right turn down a small hill and stopped by the road between the lakes. I wondered why we stopped but then realized the loud train whistle coming from Otis Summit Station meant a train would be passing by soon. I knew from my previous observations that carriages always gave way to trains to avoid collisions, so we calmly waited for the train to pass.

The horses were restless, but our driver did a good job of maintaining control. The wagon carriage rocked a little as the horses jerked and neighed in anticipation of the passing train. Smoke could now be seen as the train passed the beach, boathouse and between the lakes. No whistle blew as they passed, I was sure much appreciated by our driver. After the train had passed far enough that I could be sure Liz would hear me, I asked her about the planned events for that evening.

"I must work, but I can meet you and attend the bonfire when my chores are finished," Liz said as the wagon jerked forward and moved between the lakes. I pondered what I would do until then. "Natives will be here for a small show and dance later this evening," she continued, and I surmised it would not be as big as the "Buffalo Bill's Wild West" shows I had enjoyed at Ambrose Park in Brooklyn.

Those shows featured Indians with long, feathered headdresses on horses overtaking fast moving carriages, guns popping and expert riders and shooters performing tricks. Not wanting to sound disappointed, I told her I looked forward to seeing the show with her later that evening. The sky began to darken as we approached the hotel, and Liz said rain would reach the hotel before we would.

"When low clouds block the view of mountains in the distance, rain is only minutes away," Liz said with confidence. True to her natural senses, we stopped at the pylons on the circular drive and as I helped Liz off the wagon it began to rain. We ran holding hands, running in the drenching rain until we reached the back entrance. Soaked to our bones, we had to laugh at the situation. Patrons in the hall smiled at our obvious pleasure together. Looking out the back entrance I noticed the goats were moved again, and they appeared indifferent to the rain.

"I really enjoyed our time today at the falls, Karl," Liz said as she shook off the rain. "The bonfire and native show will begin around 9:30 PM this evening in a field past the boathouse near the band pavilion," she continued.

"Where would be the best place for us to meet later?" I inquired.

"The office here would be fine. I should be finished by then," she said as she turned to enter the office. I told her I also had a great time with her and looked forward to seeing her later. Our timing was good, as I noticed patrons beginning to mingle in the front lounge as I walked up the central staircase to my room.

I washed my face and hands in preparation for dinner, changed my shirt and shoes, sprinkled cologne on my clothes and left my room for the stairs. I checked my watch and surmised I had several minutes to enjoy the view from the portico before dinner would be served. Hoping to see a familiar face, I walked out the front entrance, down the portico steps, and walked along the iron railing near the cliff edge.

Mist and low clouds from the recent rain moved slowly down the valley and slightly obscured the view. Most of the patrons stayed on the porch due to the wet grass and ground, I presumed. Herr Strand was not in his usual place and position, but his solitary chair was sitting near the edge facing the valley below.

I noticed my dress shoes were now dirty, and I wondered if there was a shoeshine boy available. As I reached the flagpole at the South end of the hotel, I heard the rumble of chairs, and walking on the porch as patrons stood in near unison, I realized this indicated dinner was about to be served. I tried to stay on the drier pathway as I returned to the portico steps and moved toward the dining hall.

Swept up in the river of people heading to the dining hall from the front lounge, I quicky tried to decide which people near me might provide the best conversation. The stocky, bald man with a beautiful woman on his arm? Maybe the elderly gentleman who checked his bejeweled watch? Forced to sit at the next available table, my desire for controlled conversation and acquaintances was quicky deterred.

Hopefully optimistic that serendipity would rule the experience, I settled down with an interesting assortment of fellow patrons at our table. Assured by my three-day visit and gregarious personality that someone would be familiar, I swept the table with my eyes and did not recognize a single soul.

As the conversation lulled momentarily, I offered to anyone at the table, "I viewed the falls today and they were as beautiful as everyone said. Has anyone else visited the falls?"

"We have. The falls are a true natural wonder," said an elderly man sitting next to, I assumed, his wife.

"I have been fortunate to have good weather on my recent excursions to local hotels and features. However, I was caught in a sudden downpour this afternoon. I did not hear any thunder, must be ol' Rip didn't play nine-pin bowling today with Hudson's crew," I said in reference to the famous Catskill tale.

"Where are you from?" I queried, hoping to continue our conversation.

"Hans Lockemann. My wife and I are from West Hurley in Ulster County, southwest of here down in the valley. Famous for our bluestone quarries. One of the largest stones ever quarried was from there. Twenty by twenty-five feet and nine inches thick. It took eight horses to drag it over a stone tramway, and one side of a tollgate had to be taken down to get it to the river." said Mr. Lockemann.

"That's remarkable. I wonder for what it was used?" I inquired.

"Not sure. I heard it was used as part of a floor for a bank. No one digging into that vault from below," said Mr. Lockemann. Several patrons at our table snickered at that observation.

I was about to mention the bluestone shipping yard we passed on the Hudson near the Rondout Lighthouse when the doors from the kitchen burst open and once more, several black men with white jackets and gloves entered the room and brought dishes to the tables.

Too hungry to continue my personal scrutiny of the differences in dining rooms and presentations between the hotels, I scooped heartily from the delectable dishes to my plate. There were many fresh hot vegetables, steaks, ham, sliced meats such as beef and lamb, cheeses, and warm bread with butter. I finished with fresh berries and pound cake.

Our table was unusually quiet, and everyone ate heartily. I believed the mountain air, walking, and fresh, well-prepared food all contributed to our voracious appetites. As I finished and said good evening to my fellow dinner patrons, I pondered how I would spend my evening before the bonfire with Liz. My decision to play nine-pin bowling in the hotel game room was rewarded with hours of enjoyment.

However monotonous and tedious resetting the pins and returning the ball might have seemed to the hotel staff, I reminded myself there were many more strenuous and difficult assignments performed around the hotel and this was certainly not one of them. I purchased a cigar at the bar and found a comfortable chair on the portico to smoke.

A long shadow from the hotel extended over the precipice in front and the mountains in the distance glowed orange from the setting sun behind the hotel. One of the several black men waiters serving the hotel patrons asked me if I would like something to drink.

"I would appreciate water with ice, thank you," I said as I was quite parched and had not properly hydrated myself. I lit my cigar, tipped the waiter for my water, and enjoyed my smoke on the portico. A cool breeze rose from the valley and blew my smoke toward a group playing a board game nearby.

I considered moving to not disturb them with my cigar, but my entire body ached from the day's activities, and I decided the wind would change. More hotel residents came and sat at tables and benches on the porch as I continued to smoke. I checked my watch, and it was 8:30 PM. Taking advantage of the hour until I would meet Liz, I again visited the bar this time for a beer to further quench my thirst and cleanse the cigar from my palate. I hoped to meet Mr. Bannerman for our discussed beer together but was content to find a stool at the bar and drink a cold beer alone.

Soon after my first sip of a fine ale I was pleasantly surprised by a woman who purposefully sat next to me. She asked if I remembered her. Not wanting to ruin the moment with a pretty woman who started a conversation, I said, "Of course. Didn't we meet on the train?" as I attempted to hide my lack of conviction and hoped I was correct.

"Yes, we did. I was hoping to get to know you better," she said as she gently touched my arm. Her mannerisms, her perfume and clothes all led me to believe she was a woman of sophistication, I thought to myself, as I ordered another beer. The bar attendant gave me a quick wink of approval after looking at my new acquaintance. His endorsement encouraged and emboldened me to further pursue the opportunity to know her better.

"I'm sorry we haven't had the opportunity to talk. I'm Karl Debacher, an accountant from New York City," I said as I inquired about her place of residence.

"Bernadette Guettler from Yonkers. Friends call me Bernie – you may also. I work in the city likewise," she said, as I belatedly ordered her a drink. "I work for The Gillman Recruiting Agency. We help professionals find high-paying positions in the city and surrounding area. I suspected you were a professional by your level of language and professional attitude when we first met. I might be able to help you find a better position at another company," she offered. Sufficiently confused by her motivation, I wondered if she was interested in me or whether she could make money finding me a new position. I preferred to believe it was both.

We exchanged business cards, and she recognized the firm where I worked. She said she had placed people in our business, and despite a few attempts we were unable to discern a common acquaintance. We continued discussing the changes in the city and what restrictions and taxes a new President might impose on business.

She was quite knowledgeable and spoke very well. As she continued to pursue an active participation in our complex conversations I began to wonder if I should have spent my last few days with her instead of Liz. My thoughts were not alone.

"I noticed you have been courting a worker girl here at the hotel. Are you sure of her ambitions?" Bernie asked, not attempting to hide her disdain with the tone and turn of her voice. I was less sure of Bernie's intentions. I finished my beer, tipped the bar attendant, thanked her for her time and left the bar promptly. Reminded of the lack of pretentiousness of Liz and others I had met in the mountains; I realized questioning how I had spent my time was now resolved.

The Hoop Dance

The cool, clean air of the mountains called me back to the porch for a momentary respite of quiet before I met Liz. As it was time, I walked down the hall and waited while Madelyn calmly dealt with a woman who had a bee in her bonnet and was obviously upset about something at the hotel. I waited until she finished her rant and left, then attempted to commiserate with Madelyn about how difficult her job must be.

"Some days are good," Madelyn said with slight sarcasm. "Most days I enjoy it here," she continued with a smile as I entered the office to pet Sebastian. He left his basket and came to me with his head down, then rolled over to allow a little belly rub. I was pleased I had won his trust.

"He doesn't like many men, especially men he does not know. He trusts you because Liz does," Madelyn said as Liz came in through the office door and offered me a smile.

Liz carried a blanket as we walked hand-in-hand to the bonfire. The evening twilight lit our way as we passed the gardens, barns, boat dock, beach, bandstand and into an opening in the trees. While walking we discussed our day together. I inquired, "Will you visit me in New York?" She replied that it would be a dream, but she didn't have the resources to make such a trip.

"I have two weeks' time between my work here and my winter job in the Adirondacks," she said.

I had assumed she worked locally near her family in the fall and winter, possibly in hotel work of some type when the mountain hotels close.

"Do you also work at a hotel in the Adirondacks?" I asked, disappointed that she may not visit me in the city in the fall.

"I work at the Adirondack Lodge on Heart Lake. Mr. Stoeber is the proprietor there. He reminds me of Herr Strand. They have both been supportive and kind to me," she said.

"Here we are," she said as we entered the clearing. Moonlight replaced twilight and gave an odd, bluish glow to the tops of the trees and outlined the soft-looking clouds. We found a comfortable place to sit and spread our blanket on the damp ground. I looked up to see more stars than I had ever observed in my life. Orange embers from the bonfire flew into the sky and smoke occasionally obscured my heavenly view.

The audience was an interesting mix of couples, people with small children in their laps and a few elderly individuals. Obscured by the people sitting in front of us, someone near the fire pit announced simply, "The Hoop Dance" and sat down. As a very stern looking Indian pounded a steady drumbeat, the jingle of bells announced the entrance of the dancer from the left, behind the fire. A few feathers stuck out of his headband, and he had amulets on his wrist, arms, and legs. He wore a leather breechcloth around his waist and leather moccasins. A large hoop made of wood was switched from hand to hand as he stepped effortlessly through the hoop behind the fire, his movements rhythmically perfect to the drumbeat. Everyone was mesmerized as we observed his physical prowess and coordination.

His actions became more complicated as the native progressed faster through his dance stages and his feet shifted even faster to the beat. He danced around the fire, his performance dramatized by the flickering flames and rising embers filtering his dance when he was behind the fire.

When he finished the dance, his body glistened with sweat and glowed in the firelight. We applauded his efforts as he raised the hoop, and the drummer hit the drum one last hard beat. Again, someone stood near the fire and announced that anyone, especially young people, were welcome to come forward and dance with the Indians.

As a few participants accepted the offer and moved toward the front, I noticed other Indians of various ages including a few children who were sitting near the fire got up and helped the young ones to dance. One older native man gained my attention as he had a constant grin and seemed childlike in his ways. Although I observed nothing but kind gentleness in his way with the children, I commented about him to Liz and wondered about the safety of little ones near someone who was obviously different.

"I know these Indians as they come every week, year after year. He is as simple as a child and the other natives know he means no harm. They trust him completely," Liz said to ease my apprehensions.

Children danced around, as adults kept them safe from the fire. One native child passed closely enough for me to notice several small, multi-colored handprints all over his buckskin jacket. Considerate they let the child color his own clothing, I thought. Surprisingly, the intimacy of an Indian show so close and personal compared favorably to the large, distant shows of Buffalo Bill. These were not like the Indian with the full-feathered headdress on the penny in my pocket.

Neither were these natives overly dramatized as in the Buffalo Bill Cody shows I had experienced in Brooklyn. Rather, these were real people with lives and challenges like our own. Liz nudged me as I realized during my thoughts I stared at the drummer by the fire. He stared very intently at me, and I looked away as it made me uneasy.

"Mahican. He, like many of his tribe, felt betrayed by the white man. Didn't matter which side the natives took during any war here. Iroquois, Mohawk, Lenape…the government took away their land, their livelihood, but not their respect for their culture. Probably a good idea not to stare at him," Liz said with not a smidgen of sarcasm. As the show ended and people left the field for the hotel, Liz waved to her Indian friends while I folded our blanket as best as I could. I put my arm around her, and as we reached the lake in the moonlight Liz stopped and said, "See how the tree branches that hang over the lake are all the same height? No one trims them, they are trimmed by the deer in the winter. That is the highest they can reach while standing on the frozen lake."

Again, I was amazed at her knowledge of the natural world around us. A few chickens clucked as we passed the henhouse, annoyed by the light of the kerosene lanterns others carried. I noticed a few young couples giggled as they took the path toward the South Lake beach.

"We sometimes catch people swimming at the South Lake beach in the late evening. They are rarely clothed," Liz said with a smile as we continued into the hotel.

"I wish I could spend your last day here with you, but I will be busy all day tomorrow until the ball in the evening," Liz said as we said goodnight. We agreed to meet near the office as I kissed her gently and told her I would probably stay near the Mountain House tomorrow. I took the stairs to my room, washed my face and hands, undressed, lay in bed, and considered my options for my last day in the mountains. A swim, boating? More bowling or maybe billiards? I had barely begun my thoughts before I was asleep.

Pine Pillows and Rowing

Bed sheets stuck to my body in the humid morning as the now familiar bell awakened me from my deep slumber. I decided that a sunrise to start the day then dancing at the ball with Liz in the evening would be perfect bookends to the day. I joined the quiet group through the hall and down the stairs. A cleaning crew were taking a break in the front foyer. The hotel was always clean but all I ever observed was the hallway swept by one of Liz's girls.

Quietly during the late hours, a dedicated cleaning crew kept the hotel fresh, I reasoned. Our procession was not disappointed as the morning haze burned off in the sunrise. Small, low clouds swept by in the valley below as we watched the sun begin to peek over the mountains in the distance. Assured I would never forget this image before us, I looked around the portico for a familiar face. Standing alone smoking a cigarette was Mr. Schroeder, the insurance salesman from the carriage ride.

"Want a cigarette?" he said as I approached him. I declined his offer as I was sure this tactic was because he forgot my name.

"Karl Debacher. We met on the carriage ride here. You're Mr. Schroeder, correct?" I said as we sat on chairs on the porch. He was pleasantly surprised I remembered his name and asked me to call him Harold.

"Herr Strand allowed me to submit a bid on an insurance policy for his livery stable and business," Harold said with pride. "But not on the hotel itself," he added. I wanted to inquire about the estimated value of the hotel and how much it would cost to insure, but he seemed content with his business transactions with Herr Strand, so I did not inquire more. "This is my last day at the hotel. I leave tomorrow morning," Harold said.

"I will be leaving tomorrow also. Any plans for your return transportation, Harold?" I asked, as I remembered he was from Poughkeepsie, the same direction to which I would be going.

"I bought tickets at the Otis Summit," he said as he pulled the ticket out of his jacket pocket and read the details aloud.

"I take the Kaaterskill Railroad to Kaaterskill Junction, then the Stony Clove and Catskill Mountain Railroad to Phoenicia, where I take the Ulster and Delaware train to Kingston Point, then a steamship ride down and across the Hudson to Poughkeepsie." I thanked him for the information and said I would probably take the same route back to the city.

"Sure you don't want a cigarette?" Harold asked as he lit another one.

"No thank you, I only smoke cigars," I said as I began to get up from my chair.

"Breakfast is not served for a couple of hours. Why not relax out here?" Harold asked. I told him I had a long day ahead and would need to prepare. However, I knew my preparation involved going back to sleep. As we said goodbye, I congratulated him and wished him further success in his future business ventures.

"Hope to see you on the train home," Harold said sincerely and thanked me for my kind words of encouragement. The word *home* triggered a rush of mixed emotions. I missed my city life, but I knew I would miss Liz immeasurably. Conflicted in my thoughts as I climbed the stairs, I entered my room and fell back to sleep.

Awakened by voices in the hall, I washed my face and hands, changed my shirt, sprinkled some cologne on my clothes and walked down the stairs to wait in the foyer lounge for breakfast. Some activities now seemed satisfactorily routine, and I was melancholy as many actions would be the last time I experienced them before I left.

Determined to enjoy the bountiful feasts that the Catskill Mountain House called meals, I joined a table with an available seat, welcoming patrons, and several friendly faces. Being German, I tried and enjoyed the stewed kidneys, as I grew up eating blood sausage, liverwurst, and other such traditional foods. I washed down another German dish of frizzled beef and eggs with a cold glass of fresh milk and finished with corn bread topped with fresh berries and hot cups of coffee.

All was consumed while I listened attentively to the conversations at our table. One person related the story of a snake in the road which caused their carriage horses to rear up and almost upended their driver. I was especially intrigued by a conversation about items being sold by Indians near the hotel back entrance. A young couple at our table expounded about the jewelry and other objects they bought from them that morning.

Reminded that I needed to get my custom knife from the blacksmith that day, I determined to add a visit to the Indians to my itinerary. I thanked everyone at my table for their company and walked up to my room, changed into comfortable clothes, and decided to go boating.

Although I had sailed on the Hudson with friends, I had never rowed a boat on my own. I wondered why I felt the strong desire to do something physical, as I could have easily relaxed with a cigar on the portico most of the day. Maybe the Indian who performed the hoop dance inspired me to improve my physical appearance, I thought as I left my room for the staircase.

The office was remarkably busy for midweek with clientele as I passed the door on my way out the hotel back entrance. The goats were now near the south side of the hotel, and for the first time I noticed the distinct ring of the blacksmith's hammer in the distance.

Shaded by the hotel in the morning sun, I continued toward the lakes when I noticed the Indians occupied a table not far from the barns and strategically positioned in sight of patrons who disembarked the carriages near the rear pylons. Fortunately, I had the foresight before I left my room to grab money for beverages and such at the small stand by the beach.

Not wanting to miss the display, I walked to their arrangement and observed handmade beaded necklaces, leather moccasins, feathers, furs and more all laid out on a beautiful blanket with colorful intersecting patterns. Two Indian women, one young and one old were seated at the other side of the table. Small cloth sacks caught my interest, and I inquired what they were.

"Pine…pine pillows smell good," the elderly native said as she picked one up and placed it near her nose.

We agreed on a price, and I almost left before I thought Liz might appreciate a beautiful, bead and bone necklace. Would she feel pressured to wear it at the ball? Although charming, would it be formal enough for the 'Best Wednesday Night Ballroom Dance in Town'? I decided to leave that up to Liz and bought a pine pillow and a necklace.

Pleased with my decision I placed the items carefully in my pockets and enjoyed the sun on my face as I reached the boathouse. A pleasant young man there helped me push the boat onto the lake near the beach and placed the oars in the boat. The oar mechanisms were difficult to install, as I had observed other novice boaters such as myself struggle with them on the lake for the last two days.

With the oars secured to the sides of the boat, I began to methodically row the best I could around North Lake. At first my efforts were probably humorous to shoreline observers, but my rowing skills quickly improved. Although it was a small lake, I did not get halfway around the lake before my arms tired.

Exhausted but determined, I finished my brief journey and stepped into the surprisingly cold water as I waded with the boat in tow to shore. Pleased the young man at the boathouse did not comment about my short outing, he returned the boat to the boathouse, and I decided a cigar on the porch would have probably been the better choice.

The chilly lake water deterred me from the serious consideration of a swim. My trouser cuffs were wet, and I felt slightly defeated by my attempted boating excursion. Thankfully, the pine pillow and necklace were still safe in my pockets. As I left the shade of the pine trees near the lakeshore in front of the boathouse, I found a chair in the sun near the beach to warm myself.

I felt the warmth of the sun and my clothes were beginning to dry. Although I had to leave the next day, the joyfulness of children playing in the sand near me, the blue lake, the mountain scenery, the clear sky and air all contributed to my desire to stay longer and make more memories. Postcards and pictures could not capture the true beauty of the lake scenery and more I had witnessed.

I tilted my head back, closed my eyes and tried to recreate the majesty of the surrounding natural wonders I had seen. Satisfied that many scenes and experiences were now engrained in my memory, I opened my eyes and continued to enjoy the real beauty around me.

The sun was beginning to burn my skin, and afraid I would fall asleep and embarrass myself in the chair, I decided to leave and go back to the hotel and change again. The Indians were packing up their items and leaving as I passed their location; they waved and smiled at me as if we were friends. I waved in return and smiled as I noticed another carriage round the circle and stop at the pylons.

Purposefully I slowed my step to observe the people disembark from the carriage. A young girl dressed amazingly well for her age stepped out with her equally well-dressed parents into the sunlight. Three black men ran to the carriage from the hotel to get their luggage in anticipation of a hefty tip, I speculated. As the family shared a conversation and walked toward the hotel, I wanted to remember to ask Madelyn who they were.

I followed several steps behind the couple and though I wanted to linger near the office to determine their identity, Madelyn was too busy to take time to quench my curiosity about our special guests, so I continued up to my room. The fragrance of the pillow was very pleasurable as I laid the pillow and the necklace on the chest of drawers. I changed into comfortable, dry trousers and walked down the stairs to the foyer to grab a newspaper.

My desire to smoke a cigar satiated by my recent somewhat unpleasant experience, I settled into a chair in the shade on the portico and accepted Herr Strand's opinion that his customers had the best view in the Catskills. Although I appreciated the opulence of the Hotel Kaaterskill and the beauty of the falls by the Laurel House, neither hotel presented the view enjoyed by visitors and occupants of the Catskill Mountain House.

The humid haze of summer did not obscure the fields below or the slender line of the Hudson River in the distance. Just as I began to read the paper, the familiar ring of the blacksmith's hammer in the distance again reminded me to collect my knife. My enjoyment of the newspaper was pleasantly interrupted by servers who brought me the occasional lemonade.

But my peaceful respite was more disrupted by my intense curiosity, as I was determined to establish who our opulent guests were. I finished the paper, tipped my server well, and aligned my view with the center hallway well enough to notice the office at the other end of the hall did not have a queue of patrons or appear busy. Were they from Canada? I was not close enough earlier to discern their accent.

Madelyn was writing at the office desk when I entered and asked, "Who are they?" as if she had any idea. A quizzical look from her and I added, "The wealthy family that arrived recently. Sorry to be so abrupt, Madelyn, but they were an unusually elegant family." As I spoke, I realized it might have been misinterpreted that I meant the Catskill Mountain House did not attract a sophisticated clientele. "I understand this hotel has a history of important, influential and wealthy patrons," I said as Madelyn assured me no offense was taken by her. She informed me in a soft voice, "Chef Kristiansen is so annoyed. The last time those stuffy Brits the Birdwhistles stayed here they wouldn't eat his food."

"None of it?" I asked, surprised that nothing on such a voluminous menu would appeal to them.

Madelyn explained, "I exaggerate, but not only would they not eat the squash souffle they asked to see the cook. When Chef Kris, as we call him, came out to the dining hall, and asked them what was wrong they said calmly, 'Why are you serving us pig food?' in reference to the squash souffle. 'Pig food! These are the freshest vegetables in the county! What pig food?' Chef Kris said loudly as the dining hall went silent. 'This food is only good for farm animals. Take it back,' Mr. Birdwhistle said. Chef Kristiansen, a good man, took the dish back. I think you understand why he is not happy to see them. The next morning, they complained that the corn muffins were also, 'inappropriate for human consumption,' or something similar. Obviously, they were confused about our food. I was afraid to let Chef Kris know they were back. But while peeling potatoes in the kitchen he saw them through the kitchen door. After they went to their suite, I heard some pans banging and loud Norskie words he doesn't usually yell."

"Norwegian. I thought he was Swedish," I said.

"Oh no, he's a Norskie," Madelyn corrected, "We receive and employ several Norskies here at the hotel. They are the greatest people, proud of Norway and like the name Norskies. Chef Kris is a truly kind person. And he loves Sebastian."

"Where is the little guy?" I asked as I noticed he was not in his office basket.

"An animal loving little girl begged to take him on a walk with the other children today. He loves walks so I let him go. Liz's girls will make sure he is safe and gets water. They should be back soon as it is almost lunch time." A quick check of my watch let me know she was correct. I thanked Madelyn for satiating my curiosity about our special guests and said goodbye.

As I walked down the hall, I noticed patrons were shuffling into the dining room, so I joined the stream of people. I hardly had a chance to introduce myself to another table of strangers when from my angle in the room, I was fortunate enough to notice the Birdwhistle family being regally treated and seated by the eager staff at their own table.

Servers wiped down each chair and stood at attention near the family. Their table was served first and at once, with every dish brought to Mr. Birdwhistle for his nod of approval before being served to each family member. Intrigued by the level of detail afforded the Birdwhistle family, I tried to remember when I had seen such fawning in public in the city. None came to mind just as our table was served the usual variety of wonderful, delectable sustenance.

Sliced smoked beef with Worcestershire Sauce, potato salad, sliced cucumbers and tomatoes, and a few cups of coffee completed my desired satisfaction for another good meal at the hotel. Our table was unusually quiet I thought. Was the reason I was too preoccupied with the sycophantic acts nearby to try to direct our conversation? Whatever the reason, determined for some type of discourse before we left the table, I asked who would be at the ball that evening. Numerous affirmative responses led me to believe it was significant and might be fully attended.

My dancing skills did not match my piano playing ability, and I worried I might be more likely to bump into or step on someone in a crowded ballroom. I wished everyone a good afternoon. As I left the dining hall, I noticed Mr. Birdwhistle stood and handed out money to a line of servers while his family rose from the table.

I knew some wealthy people in my accounting business, but I never really appreciated how wealth could bring as much trouble as pleasure. I felt sorry for the expectations that Mr. Birdwhistle was required to meet in every interaction merely because of his wealth. But he should have tried Chef Kris' corn muffins.

Otis Railway Summit Station and Saratoga Chips

Otis Elevating Railroad summit

Unsure of the demand for tickets for my desired mode of transportation back to the city, I decided to prioritize procuring my train ticket to Kingston and proceeded to the Otis Summit Station. As I walked toward the hotel back door, I noticed our coach driver Greg unloading suitcases from a wagon. Several black servers carried the suitcases inside the hotel as I stepped out into the sunlight and asked Greg if he could provide a ride to the Otis Summit Station.

"Good to see you again, sir," Greg said politely and indicated it would be fine to ride to the station. The servers finished unloading the wagon and Greg offered me the front seat with him as before.

"How do they know where to place the suitcases?" I asked as we pulled away from the hotel and headed West toward the barns and lakes.

"Mrs. Schumacher marks the luggage tags with your name. Maddy matches your name with the room registry and marks the ticket. Your bag was probably in your room before you, as I saw that you walked to the hotel," Greg said as we took a trail that curved by the lakes and brought us past the North Lake beach to the station.

"Did the lady have difficulty walking on the gravel road?" Greg asked with sincerity.

"She did fine. She is tough and didn't complain," I said as our wagon pulled up to the station's two-story landing by the tracks. A locomotive loudly spewed occasional steam and appeared to be ready to depart. I tipped Greg and said goodbye as he took control of the wagon and headed back toward the hotel. A sign indicated that tickets were available upstairs at the station office on one side of the tracks.

Otis Summit Railway Station and Power House

The other side of the station, close to where the Otis Elevating Railway reached the top of the incline, had a building attached with a sign indicating it was the power house. Several people were standing watching the train by the railing on the second level by the ticket office. I entered the office and let them know my destination and desired transportation by train and then ship.

"We don't sell no river boat tickets here, just the train tickets," the ticket booth attendant barked loudly at me through the ticket window. "You get them at Kingston Point near Rondout," the attendant continued. I purchased my ticket and noticed the destinations listed were the ones previously identified by Harold. The towns and stops had interesting names such as Kaaterskill Junction, Stony Clove, and Phoenicia.

"Would it be possible to see the mechanics of the Otis Elevating Railway across the tracks?" I asked the booth attendant.

"Sure. Jules will show you around if he's not too busy." I thanked him and walked down the steps and across the tracks in front of the steam spouting locomotive.

At the top of a set of stairs past some barrels of fuel I passed a building with a tall smokestack labeled 'Power House'. That side of the tracks was much more utilitarian, with iron railings and narrow walkways, unlike the wide walkways, wooden railings, awnings, and benches on the other ticket booth side. My curiosity overcame my discomfort as I wandered areas I certainly did not belong, and I walked through a door into a large, tall room that was perched at the top of the Otis Elevating Railway precipice.

A large white pipe came through the wall and connected with two mechanical devices with pulleys and smaller pipes which appeared to be steam engines. These engines were on either side of two ten-foot-high spoked metal wheels which dominated most of the room's available space. The immense wheels were geared and worked in tandem with the steam power to pull a large cable that went through a gap in the wall.

A man sat writing or reading at a small desk on the other side of the room with his back to the door and did not see me enter. Although the wheels were not moving, there were enough mechanical noises in the room to cover the sound of my entrance. I did not want to startle him, and I did not recognize the echo potential of the room when I somewhat loudly announced my presence.

"Hello, sir, sorry to bother you." He turned in his chair and smiled.

"No bother at all," he said as he rose from his chair, put out his cigarette and limped past the giant wheels to greet me.

"You must be Jules. The ticket booth attendant said you wouldn't mind my interest if you were not too occupied to accommodate," I said as we shook hands. His leg appeared stiff as if in a cast and he did not bend the knee. "If you're not too busy, I'd like to understand how this all works," I asked with sincere interest as I waved my hand toward the wheels and pipes.

"Yes, the name's Jules. Dad loved Jules Verne's books, so he named me after the author. Anyway, when this bell rings, I know it is time to start the cable that makes everything happen," Jules said as he pointed to a bell on a wall next to a platform. On the stand were three levers with handles which could be operated while standing. A window on the wall in front of the platform allowed the operator to see the railway cars down the mountainside.

"These levers control the engagement of the two Hamilton Corliss steam engines that power the large wheels connected to a cable. A single cable moves the rail cars up and down the mountain side. A rail car ascends at the same time another rail car is descending. Since the cars share the same center rail and cable, the cars pass each other in a bow in the tracks halfway down the incline. Although the railway is steep, it is completely safe. We have passenger, open-air luggage, and freight rail cars. Every railway car has an emergency brake that will stop the car if anything goes wrong. If the cars are moving too fast or the cable disconnects the brake will mechanically engage. Also, a conductor rides in every car and can throw a brake if needed. We have never had any problems with this system. I helped build this line," Jules shared proudly. His knowledge of the system was impressive. Obviously, he was more than an operator and inhabited the position of engineer.

"Thank you for your time and patience explaining all this. I will not take any more of your time. I regret not taking the Otis Railway. My back is still sore from the carriage ride up the mountain days ago," I shared as we said goodbye. It was difficult for me to remember the initial impression of the Otis Elevating Railway I imagined before I left New York on vacation. Visions of choking in smoke as a train climbed up a steep mountainside were unwarranted as this was a safe and clean form of transportation. The experience of the carriage ride and meeting interesting passengers did not outweigh the discomfort I would have missed had I taken the Otis Railway.

I found my way back to the tracks and the conductor waved for me to cross in front of the large black, steam locomotive. I continued up the stone covered incline back toward the hotel. Certain that I had enough money with me to reimburse the blacksmith for my knife, I proceeded to his shop by a path on the north end of the hotel.

The ringing of his hammer on the anvil from a distance assured me that he would be present for the transaction. Several working girls with their distinctive blue and white dresses were walking toward the hotel and passed by me on the trail. I heard mumblings about Liz and assumed they recognized me, although in their similar dress, age, and hair styles I doubt I could separate one girl from another even if introduced.

Black soot settled on my shirt from the smoke that bellowed out of the chimney of the blacksmith shop. As I entered, I was careful not to trip as last time and avoided the bricks that stopped the door from swinging inward. I said hello to Hank who was sitting on a chair near a horse, and he waved and said hello in my direction. Having heard our exchange, Victor, the blacksmith, stopped hammering and took off his leather gloves and smock to greet me.

"Mr. Derbacker, correct?" Victor asked.

Not sure if I should correct him, I said, "Debacher. But that is fine. Good to see you. I'm looking forward to seeing my knife."

"Let me get it," Victor said as he went to a table under several tools hanging on a wall to our right and returned with the knife wrapped in a brown rag. He unwrapped the burlap cloth to reveal a large knife with a white bone handle.

"It is sharp. A dull knife is useless. I would store it in an oil cloth like this to keep it nice." Victor said as he wrapped up then handed the knife to me. I thanked him for his fine work and paid him more than we agreed as an expression of my gratitude. I thanked him again and said our goodbyes. Hank said, "Be careful. It's sharp."

I thanked Hank for the advice, wished him well and walked back into the afternoon sunlight. The cloth had an oily smell to it, and I was determined to find a box or something in which to keep the knife from adding a permanent undesirable odor to my suitcase and clothes on my return trip. I returned to the hotel and observed the usual clientele activities of strolling couples, children playing and elderly shading themselves on the portico drinking tea and lemonade.

After a quick nod to a few somewhat familiar faces on the porch I walked up the stairs to my room. It was now after three o'clock and I decided to take a rest to ensure an energetic evening at the ball. The knife safely placed on the chest of drawers next to the pine pillow and necklace, I removed my shoes, laid down and soon was asleep.

I awoke in time for dinner and washed up while I contemplated the exciting evening to come. I dried my face and hung the towel on the portable tub I was convinced I would never get the opportunity to use. I checked my suit and realized it could have used a pressing but convinced myself it would look fine for the ball.

Concerned that anyone, especially a curious child, could gain access to my knife, I checked that I had my key and locked my door. I proceeded down the stairs and waited in the foyer with my fellow patrons. This was my last dinner at the hotel, and I was determined to control as much as was possible with whom to be associated and mingle with interesting clientele at my table. My final decision was to socialize with a jovial young couple and their friends nearby. We all walked together into the dining hall as we began to talk about the hotel and its accommodations.

"I have been here for a few days. The hotel is accommodating, and the view is spectacular. Having visited the Hotel Kaaterskill and Laurel House I appreciate the view from here even more. However, each hotel has its own unique charm, and the falls are worth the visit. Have you had a chance to explore the Overlook Hotel?" I asked one of the young gentlemen as we all sat down together.

"Willa and I took a carriage ride to the Overlook Hotel near Woodstock. The flying insects there were annoying and there was not much to see. A hotel on a rocky ledge with an elegant parlor and a nice view. It was not worth the long carriage ride," he offered as the food began to arrive.

"I wonder why people stay at the Overlook Hotel. Did you find anything distinct that might make it attractive, such as a better menu, services, game courts or other reasons?" I asked with sincere interest.

"Not that we experienced," he said with conviction. With my strong personal desire to never miss something of interest, I was satisfied I had explored the best of the surrounding region with Liz. Based upon their related experience I did not feel slighted having missed a visit to the Overlook Hotel.

Unable to resist the enormous steaks that passed when the food arrived, I resisted the mashed potatoes in favor of a peculiar, thinly cut bowl of potato slices so popular at our table I was sure there would be none for my consumption.

Overlook Mountain House, Woodstock, New York

As these potato slices looked particularly delicious, it was difficult to not be rude and scoop them all onto my plate. I heard someone at the table mention 'Saratoga Chips'.

"Did I hear you say these are called 'Saratoga Chips'?" I inquired, hoping they would not find me rude having overheard their discussion.

"We're James and Rosalyn from Malta near Saratoga. As we understand the local legend, 'Saratoga Chips' were invented at a restaurant on Saratoga Lake in Saratoga Springs by a man named Crum. A patron asked for a thinner, less soggy French fry, so the owner, George Crum, sliced the potatoes very thinly and fried them until crisp. They are quite popular, and he sells them by the box from his restaurant," proudly explained a young man at our table.

I ate a chip and was surprised by its crisp texture and salty taste.

"They are quite interesting. I'm surprised I haven't seen them before," I said, confused in my pretentiousness that everything wasn't either invented or perfected in New York City.

"They're sold in stores also. Of course, it is mostly a name, and the chips are made and sold in many places now," said Rosalyn. I thoroughly enjoyed my chips and considered asking our servers for more.

"I have friends who visit the Saratoga Race Track in the summer to gamble on the horse races all the way from New York City," I shared with my table mates, as the name Saratoga finally jogged my memory for the familiarity of the race course. I chose not to share that my friends noted a decline in the quality of the Saratoga facility over the years, as it had become an attraction for objectionable participants in their estimation. Also, there had been excitement and anticipation about a new track being established in Brooklyn.

The absence of attentive detail afforded our refined patrons from England caused me to overlook their lack of attendance at the meal. As I contemplated where the Birdwhistles chose to dine, I was pleasantly surprised to be served fresh berries which accompanied a few graham wafers and coffee and finished my meal quite satisfactorily.

I thanked my fellow dinner patrons for their time and fine conversation. I also wished them a pleasant time on their mountain journeys, as I mentioned mine were finished and I would be leaving the next day. They wished me a safe trip and we said goodbye. As I left the dining hall, I turned to observe that the servers' lack of enthusiasm was probably a reflection of disappointment that the Birdwhistle's senior patron was not dolling out cash that evening.

The Ball

Concerned that my suit for the Ball needed to be pressed to look my best, I stopped at the office and asked Maddy if there was any way to get my suit pressed and my shoes shined.

"Bring me the suit and I'll have one of the girls iron out the creases. The best I can do is offer you the hotel shoe shine kit and you can shine them yourself. Please use the buffing cloth included with the kit. Herr Strand gets angry when patrons stain his towels with shoe shine," Maddy let me know.

I assured her I would respect the hotel linens and proceeded to my room to get my suit. I passed several young people in the hall who were jolly enough to be at least slightly inebriated. I hoped people at the ball later in the evening would be respectful enough to withhold their selfish desire to drink to excess and potentially ruin the event for others. I determined that no matter what happened around us, Liz and I would have a memorable evening together.

My suit in hand, I locked my door and brought the apparel to the office where Maddy had already assigned a young girl to iron my clothes. She left the office with my suit, and I found a comfortable chair near Maddy's desk to wait. I decided to ask Maddy an important question.

"How long have you known Liz?" I asked, hoping Maddy did not think I was too forward.

"We have worked here three summers together. I know her well," Maddy assured me.

"You know Liz and can tell I care very much for her. I just want your assurance that she is sincere in her affection for me. I guess I just don't know how this relationship will proceed," I said without trying to sound too distressed. I realized I might have put too much pressure on Maddy as she quietly left the room, returned, and handed me a well-worn shoe shine kit. It was a simple box with many stains and dark fingerprints on every side. As she handed me the box it rattled inside.

"You are special to her. Men have approached her for her attention, and she has dated infrequently. My knowledge of her actions at this hotel for the past three years is good. We share our thoughts and dreams like sisters. Trust me, you are the one she wants and loves."

Her words finally eased my apprehensions about Liz's sincerity. I told her I was grateful for her honesty. The girl returned from across the hall with my suit; I thanked her and tipped her well. The office started to become busy with people checking into the hotel, so I thanked Maddy for her help and promised to return the shoe shine kit.

Not wanting anyone to observe me perform such a rudimentary process in public, I brought the kit back to my room and proceeded to improve my shoes. The box contents were more than sufficient to complete the task, and I was reminded by the smell of the polish of the many times I was required to reluctantly perform the ritual as a child on Saturday evening to be properly attired for church on Sunday.

As I was annoyed to have to perform the task again, the reason for the excessive importance I placed on shined shoes was suddenly evident. The logic, however flawed from my childhood, was if I had to have shined shoes, why didn't everyone else have shined shoes? Satisfied that I would not be the worst dressed at the ball, I laid my suit on the bed, left my room, and walked to the ballroom to see how it was decorated for the evening.

The sound of a band practicing became louder as I stood near the doorway and watched the progress. Servers were attaching bunting between the windows on the courtyard side, while others prepared tables and swept floors. The white curtains on the French balcony doors I had observed during a previous dance were replaced with a beautiful floral pattern that matched the tablecloths.

I was determined to remember to ask Liz if Jackie was the seamstress responsible for this colorful display. I checked my watch and surmised I had about an hour before I needed to get ready for the ball. The piano was unoccupied, and I was tempted but not audacious enough to ask to play along with the band while they practiced. My curiosity led me to wonder what Liz was doing to get ready, and when would be the appropriate time to give her the necklace?

I left the ballroom and returned the shoe shine box to Maddy in the office. As I placed it on a table behind her desk and thanked her, I noticed a few carved wooden animals in a box and inquired about them.

"Hank carves them for the children. Wonderful, aren't they?" Maddy said as I picked up a toy horse and marveled at the detail considering he had no sight. "You can take one if you want. Hank from the blacksmith shop carves them all the time," Maddy offered but I declined, as I felt uncomfortable taking a toy meant for the hotel children. I thanked her again for her help, left the office and stopped to check my watch. Nervous that however I chose to spend the next hour I did not want to be so preoccupied that I would be late to the ball, I decided to watch patrons from the portico.

I walked down the stairs and passed a young couple who were very well dressed, I assumed, for the ball. My excitement for the evening was not abated by the mundane observation of the older gentlemen playing checkers next to my seat on the portico. A gentle, cool breeze came up from the valley and moved the cigarette smoke around the porch in swirls. More well-dressed young patrons walked by the front of the hotel, and again my thoughts were about Liz and an evening of dancing.

A group of young children ran by the porch, and one of them came up the stairs and asked if she could hide behind my chair for their game. I obliged her request, and she was briefly successful as a few children came to the top of the stairs, looked around, and left unfulfilled in their quest. A few minutes later they returned to find her crouching behind me.

All giggles and laughter ensued as they gently grabbed her arm and led her off the porch. Their young energy and excitement in play was both palpable and enjoyable to observe. My thoughts drifted to a day too soon when I would be back at work tallying numbers at a desk in a stuffy office. But more importantly I would be without Liz. Would my work and reconnecting with the city lull me back into a comfortable life alone? I was desperate to abate my apprehension we might drift apart over our time away from each other.

However, these thoughts were too melancholy to dwell upon on such a special evening. I checked my watch and decided to return to my room and get ready for the evening. I washed my face, put on my suit and shoes, splashed on some cologne, and admired my presentation in the mirror. Pleased I did not forget it, I placed the necklace carefully in my suit pocket.

With half an hour until the ball began, I decided to mingle with patrons near the bar. The bar was across the hall from the office, consequently I believed it was the best place to meet with Liz and spend some time together before the ball. The bar was very busy and loud. When I had the opportunity, I ordered a soda in a glass as I did not want to smell like alcohol when we met.

While perusing pictures on the bar's walls, I had barely taken a sip of my drink when I felt a substantial tug at my sleeve. I turned to see Liz smile as she twirled in her elegant dress of pink with white lace and trim. Her hair up and subtle makeup done perfectly, she looked beautiful.

"Jackie made the dress. Isn't it pretty?" Liz said. I had trouble responding immediately, as I was startled by her sudden entrance and enthralled by her appearance. The energy and excitement of her entrance and twirl caught the eye of several bar patrons.

"You look beautiful, Liz," I responded. "Jackie is an amazing seamstress," I continued.

"I am truly blessed to have such a good friend. She heard me mention I needed a dress and made this," Liz said with astonishment as she held out the dress to show the fine needlework and detail. "A root beer," she replied when I asked her if she would like something to drink from the bar. Liz held my arm as several men gazed at her while we moved through the crowd to order drinks. I felt fortunate having Liz on my side, her natural beauty and honest smile lit the room.

"The bar's crowded and the ball starts in about half an hour. Let's take our drinks and go for a short walk," I said to Liz, and she agreed. She followed my lead toward the front of the hotel, down the porch steps and along the walkway near the iron railing.

"Would you rather not go for a walk? I did not think of getting the dress dirty," I said as I noticed her lifting her hem carefully as we walked.

"Oh no, I'm fine. It's difficult to sit in a dress like this anyway," she said to assuage my guilt at my preference to go walking. I welcomed her calm demeanor and leaned in for a kiss. She obliged.

"I wanted to kiss you in the bar when you came in. You were radiant and attracted the attention of more than a few patrons. I was pleased you were with me," I said proudly. Liz shyly looked at the ground and said she appreciated the compliment.

We reached the flagpole and turned around back toward the front of the hotel. As she appeared uncomfortable being the only subject of conversation, I said, "I met Jules at the Otis Summit Station. He was very patient and showed me how the railway machinery works. I hope I didn't bother him with my questions and curiosity."

"Jules is a nice man. He was injured by a falling bridge beam during the Otis Railway construction last year. The Otis company trained him and gave him the job because he doesn't have to walk very much to control the system. I heard he's told friends he was tired of construction. Obviously, he would have preferred to get the job another way as he was severely injured. He loves his work and I'm sure you were not a bother," Liz said.

"I know you've been working at the hotel for years, but despite the number of employees you appear to know everyone who works here. How is that so?" I asked, as it did seem unusual that she knew everyone.

"Herr Strand has us all meet at the beginning of the season. Each employee is encouraged to introduce themselves and explain their position. We then have fruit punch and sandwiches in the Dining Room and get to know each other better then. It is a relaxed and smart way to meet."

"Smart is true. I'm excited to be with you tonight and dance at the ball, and I will miss you very much after I leave tomorrow. I hope you consider visiting me in New York," I said hoping to get a positive response. She hesitated and did not respond. As she looked down, discouraged, I supposed it was because she did not have the money for such a trip.

"When I asked you before about a city visit you said something about resources. If it is a matter of money...".

She turned toward me, took both my hands, quietly interrupted, and said, "I could never impose upon you in such a manner as to ask for money. The memories of us here will probably fade in your mind after you return to the city. But my continued work at this hotel after you leave will remind me every day of our time spent together here. To be with you this fall and experience the city would be wonderful. I've wanted to visit New York for years, but I simply don't have the money and rarely the time to complete the trip."

"My memory of you and our experiences will not fade, not even a little. I'll write to you often and hope you will also share your experiences as I care for you very much," I said, hoping to convince her of my sincerity. "Let's not dwell on your visit to New York anymore. Just consider that I would gladly wire you the trip money anytime," I offered before I considered there may not be a Western Union office anywhere near where she lived.

I checked my watch and realized it was after 8:00 PM and the ball had begun.

"Is there anything you need before we walk up to the ballroom?" I asked as I suddenly and fortunately remembered to give her the necklace.

"I have a gift for you. The Indians were selling these and I thought you might like it. Don't feel pressured to wear it this evening if you..." I continued as she excitedly interrupted me.

"How sweet of you. Of course, I'll wear it this evening. Please help me to put it on," she said with a smile as she twirled around, and I tied it around her neck. She touched her necklace and gave me a kiss. "Time to dance at the ball."

We lined up with other participants in the hallway on the second floor. Fashionably dressed men in their suits and women in their ball gowns discussed in excited voices about their favorite dance or how others were dressed. After noticing Liz's necklace, I noticed a woman several feet from us touch her neck and mention something to her escort. I assumed she was commenting about the jewelry.

With her strong will and sense of self, I doubt Liz would have been bothered if someone judged her attire. Never had I imagined that my last evening here at the hotel would be so interesting and rewarding. More importantly, I did not expect to find love.

With her arm in mine, we stepped up to the desk outside the ballroom where a young woman handed Liz a dance card and a small pencil. With a string tied through a hole punched in one corner, Liz slipped the card over her wrist. To be sure of the order of dances I was handed a card also, which I quickly perused to be sure of which dances I was familiar with, and when they would occur during the evening.

The front cover of the card listed the location and date, as well as the names of the "Floor Managers". Inside was the "Order of Dances", and the back listed the "Order of Engagements" where the woman or an admirer could write in the name of the dance partner for each dance by number.

The waltz was my best dance, and I was pleased to note that there were several opportunities on the schedule to demonstrate my prowess. As we entered the ballroom, numerous couples lined up to perform the "Grand March". Although I was familiar with the dance, we noticed attendees were quickly filling the tables that lined the wall near the windows to watch them perform.

We found an available table and sat with an agreeable-looking elderly couple. They smiled and nodded at us as I helped Liz into her chair. After the participants finished the "Grand March" followed by polite applause, Liz and I held hands at the table and talked about our plans for the evening.

"Can I simply pencil you in for all the dances? I'd rather spend the evening with you," she said, gazing lovingly into my eyes. Touched by her sincere affection and desire to be with me only, I touched her hand across the table.

"You are the prettiest woman here. I'm sure men this evening desire to dance with you, and I would not be intimidated by their requests. You have made it obvious I am your true love. Enjoy the evening." Liz blushed at my compliment and thanked me for my honesty. I asked Liz for her dance card and entered my name next to every waltz.

A short, balding man I had observed moving from table to table asking to be "penciled in" on the dance cards of several women grasped the opportunity to get his name on Liz's card the moment it was off her wrist. She obliged the gentleman, and he seemed delighted she wrote "John Spitzer" on the line next to two polkas listed on the program. Another gentleman stopped by and requested she participate in "The Quadrille Dance", but she respectfully declined.

Liz affirmed my request to get her a drink of punch. The refreshment table had bowls of fruit punch served in crystal glasses. When I returned with our drinks, I noticed she looked a little flushed and although I did not want to lose our table, we agreed to walk to the rear porch to enjoy the evening summer breezes. She held my arm as we walked past the colorful curtains flowing inside the French doors that opened to the back of the hotel. The four pillars identical to the pillars on the front portico framed our view of the dark red and orange colors from the sunset that seeped through the distant clouds over the mountains.

Sunset on North Lake, Haines Falls, New York

We enjoyed our drinks and toasted to us.

"I was worried. You were glowing a little too much in there," I said with a concerned voice.

"I'm fine. Just a little hot in there," she said as we sat in chairs along the wall facing west and enjoyed the view. Voices could be heard as people entered and departed the hotel below us, buckboards loaded with supplies were lined up at the rear entrance and I could smell the cigarettes of the omnipresent workmen who leaned on the wall near the door and smoked.

Liz stared wistfully straight ahead into the distance.

"I miss only being here in the summer. Sometimes I wonder how quiet, empty, lifeless, and lonely this hotel must be in the winter with no one here and snow throwing a cold, quiet cover on everything. I wonder how the gardens I tend look in the spring, when everything flowers and the grass turns green. I miss fall here, although I get to experience the beautiful colors of autumn in the Adirondacks."

I told her I had similar thoughts earlier in the week, as there would be an intense contrast between the busy, active daily activities and the cold, lifeless pall of winter. Although I wanted to further discuss the possibility of her visiting me in New York City, I sensed her previous lack of comfort and how she seemed to avoid the conversation.

Not content to leave before the issue was resolved, I nonetheless decided to live in the moment and enjoy the wonderful evening. The last light of evening gave her a glow that added to her beauty in her delightful dress. I told her she looked lovely and leaned in for a kiss which she obliged. I could hear the music for "The Quadrille Dance" and knew from my dance card that "The Polka Dance" was next.

"Let's not keep Mr. Spitzer waiting. The polka will start soon," I said, getting up to take her hand. We walked back in through the porch doors into the ballroom where Mr. Spitzer was standing alone near the windows checking his dance list. Pleased to notice Liz enter the ballroom, Mr. Spitzer walked toward us as we stood and joined a small group observing the current dancers on the floor.

Liz smiled, leaned in to get my ear and said, "The Quadrille" reminds me of the square dances we have in our barn in Cairo. Except we dance barefoot on a dirt floor. People here are dressed a little better," she said in a whimsical manner as she leaned into me and cuddled my arm.

His timing impeccable, Mr. Spitzer sauntered to Liz, politely bowed, and held out his hand for hers just as "The Quadrille Dance" ended. Liz gently squeezed my hand and gave me a reassuring look as she curtsied, and they walked onto the dance floor and claimed their position. Assuming the correct stance, I watched as he placed his hand on her back, she rested her arm on his arm and placed her hand on his shoulder, and they clasped fingers in each other's hands.

Despite his small stature, when "The Polka Dance" music started he led skillfully as they spun around the dance floor with enthusiasm. His prowess on display, Mr. Spitzer was an excellent dancer. His swift feet and remarkable command of the dance floor led several women to check their dance cards, I assumed, to see if Mr. Spitzer would be an exciting aspect of their evening.

Liz never caught my eye during the dance, but I was certain she was aware of the interest in the room. The music ended, Mr. Spitzer bowed, Liz curtsied and returned to me more flushed than earlier but certainly delighted with the dance.

We smiled at each other and decided to walk back on the porch as the music for "Les Lanciers" began. Liz found a chair and seemed pleased to rest. As I entered the ballroom to get her something to drink, I saw Mr. Spitzer near the refreshments table and congratulated him on his dancing skills. Surprised by my acknowledgement, he thanked me and commented that Liz did well also.

I returned with our drinks and was pleased that Liz had returned to a more natural color. The hotel lights attracted many flying insects, and it was difficult to maintain a conversation without the occasional swat at the annoying little biting fiends. We toasted ourselves again with our punch glasses.

"Our first waltz follows 'Les Lanciers'. I think it best for us to wait for a later waltz. The air is much fresher out here," I said as a light breeze passed between the porch columns and cooled the portico. I glanced at my dance card and reminded Liz there were several dances before Intermission.

As Liz drank her punch, I pulled a chair next to her. I touched her arm, and she rested her head gently on my shoulder.

"I loved dancing the polka, but I agree. I think it best if we wait for our waltz until after intermission," she said, as we both gazed out at the stars between the clouds.

In no hurry to return to the stuffy ballroom, I nonetheless was anxious to dance with Liz. Whatever would be our future, it didn't matter then because we were together that evening, enjoying a beautiful, unforgettable evening of romance, dance, and the company of one another.

"When you are in the Adirondacks, what are Pol, your sister and parents doing here in the Catskills?" I inquired, always curious about people and their occupations but specifically interested in getting to know Liz and her family better.

"Erin has her goats to tend. Pol brings wood up the mountain trails all winter by oxcart to the Kaaterskill Hotel to supply the next season's steam laundry needs. He also cuts ice out of the lakes, packs the large cubes in hay and delivers it to ice warehouses all winter. Or, at least when the ice is thick enough," she said, hopefully understanding my desire to get to know her and her family better and not to pry.

"Mom and dad have slowed down recently, but mom still cooks and cleans as always. Dad stopped farming and leases our land to other farmers. His passion now is to correct all the house clocks by the church bells in town," she said in a comical tone. "How do you spend your time in the winter in New York City?" Liz asked.

"Winter obviously forces us to be inside more, which I believe encourages a desire to be closer and more sociable with friends and family. Sitting by a fireplace, playing games, and drinking hot toddies. I am not one to seek many outdoor activities in winter. However, sometimes I go skating with friends in Central Park," I said as she continued to rest comfortably on my shoulder. When the music for the waltz began, I put my arm around her, and we gently swayed to the beat. I briefly closed my eyes and pictured us dancing together as people watched while I swept Liz around the ballroom.

"There is another 'Quadrille Dance' after this waltz and then Intermission. What would your perfect evening agenda be?" I asked in a teasing but loving tone. Liz glanced at her dance card tied to her wrist.

"I look forward to dancing the waltz with you. There are two waltzes after Intermission, including the last dance of the evening. How nice," she said in her usual causal style. We continued to sit quietly on the porch, as a few participants wandered out for the quick tip of a flask, or a smoke, or to be able to converse more easily than in the crowded ballroom.

We resumed our discussion about her family and her responsibilities at the Adirondack hotel.

"I know how to fit someone with snowshoes," she said proudly. "The French from Canada call snowshoes *'raquettes',*" she continued.

"Sometimes snow in New York City can shut down businesses for days. When it melts, many streets become a muddy mess. But I love it when the first snowfall softens the city in a blanket of white and the carriages are quieter in the smooth snow as they pass my apartment building," I said as we snuggled closer in the evening breeze. The music for the waltz ended and "The Quadrille Dance" began.

"I've talked to Stu about winters here at the hotel. He hunts deer, bear, turkey, ruffed grouse…whatever he can find in a season. Only a few Indians know the woods around here better than him. Stu told me about a time a terrible snow storm surprised him, and he had to break into the hotel and burn furniture for warmth. He paid Herr Strand for any damage and the furniture," Liz said, and the thought made me shiver a little in the cool summer evening breeze.

"A few locals use the larger trails in winter for horseback riding and skijoring. Ice is taken from the lakes when they can. Herr Strand said he rides a sleigh and inspects the hotel a few times in the winter when possible. But most of the winter no one is in this area," she said as the music flowed out the ballroom French doors onto the porch.

"What is skijoring?" I asked, intrigued.

"A horse pulls a skier on a rope. I've never tried it, although I've seen people skijoring down the streets of Cairo when conditions are good," she explained.

"So, there is no caretaker for the hotel in the winter?" I asked, surprised that such an investment would remain unchecked for months.

"A few caretakers from Haines Falls are paid to regularly check the hotel. They were the ones who found the damage by Stu. He had left a note, however, taking full responsibility for his actions. I have lived in the mountains my entire life. I know there are weeks when this hotel is inaccessible due to the weather," she said with unquestionable certainty. Still, I would be concerned about possible vandalism and theft, I thought.

The music to "The Quadrille Dance" ended and the noise level from the ballroom significantly increased as people felt more comfortable to converse during the Intermission. I stood and helped Liz up from her chair and we walked holding hands into the ballroom. People were talking and spreading out on the dance floor as the hotel staff brought sandwiches and desserts to the refreshment table. A slow but steady stream of participants walked to the table to view their choices.

Impressed by the politeness and courtesy everyone showed each other, we walked to the table and picked up some cake and more punch. A few people were noticeably inebriated, but they appeared to not cause any problems. All seating was taken, so I asked Liz if she would like to take our refreshments and walk to the front portico as I had seen other patrons heading in that direction.

She agreed and we found a place to lean on the front railing and enjoy our refreshments. Still astonished at the amount of effort it took to maintain the hotel, thoughts wandered to the extra work to decorate the ballroom, set up for the musicians, and make the fresh cake I was eating.

"Who is the baker in the hotel?" I asked, as I assumed it was a specialty profession.

"Chef Kris can cook anything. He is a good teacher and trains his crew well. Although each kitchen staff member usually performs specific tasks, he trains them to be well rounded cooks. Because of Chef Kris' reputation, Maddy says we get more applications for employment in the kitchen than any other positions in the hotel," Liz said to my surprise.

"Is it because he has a history of training people in a valued profession?" I asked with continued curiosity.

"Probably, I would assume. Although I believe a share of the reason is the kitchen staff has more breaks than anyone else here," she said without a hint of resentment or disdain. "I see the kitchen team between meals and frequently during the day talking and smoking outside. Chef Kris is a strict leader, but they can complete their chores and still have time to relax. Other employees making deliveries or watching the children and so on do not get to rest during their routine. Besides, anyone can deliver a slab of beef on an oxcart. Learning to cook that meat properly takes training that Chef Kris is willing to provide."

Having been afforded the opportunity to attend fine schools for accounting, I was pleased to believe there were opportunities offered here for potentially less fortunate individuals. I wanted to ask Liz if any members of her family such as Pol had considered working with Chef Kris but decided it might be considered rude or judgmental.

"Would there be similar opportunities here? For example, in the blacksmith shop?" I asked as we returned inside and walked back to the ballroom.

"I'm not sure if Victor would welcome an apprentice. But there are other opportunities here," she said as we entered the ballroom, and the music for "Les Lanciers" began. We returned our dishes to the proper table, and I thanked the busy girls who were working to keep everything in order. Liz, of course, thanked them by name.

I thought I heard one of the girls say to the other,

"She might not be 'Miss' Liz much longer," and they giggled at the prospect.

I reminded Liz that the next dance was our waltz. She hugged my arm as we watched them dance the "Les Lanciers". Like "The Quadrille Dance", the dances involve groups of four couples facing each other to form a square. There are five tours or figures of the dance, each one more complicated than the previous and performed four times apiece so each couple gets to lead the tour. I realized my love for the waltz is in its simplicity.

"Are you having a nice time?" I asked as I put my arm around her and pulled her closer.

"I'm having a wonderful time. I hope you are as good a dancer as you said you are," she said with a smile in a teasing manner.

"I've tried 'The Quadrille Dance' but have never attempted 'Les Lanciers'. I'm afraid to miss something and be embarrassed. Too many steps to remember," I said as dancers swept close to us standing at the edge of the ballroom. I wasn't sure the number of tours that were left, but confident I was ready for our waltz.

The "Les Lanciers" finished to a round of pleasant applause. We assumed our position on the dance floor. I placed her hand in mine and placed my hand on her back. She rested her arm on mine and gently touched my shoulder as we both smiled. The waltz began and she followed my lead perfectly. As we swept across the dance floor, I became more confident in my steps and enjoyed watching the smiles of other dancers as we passed them. Liz gazed at me only, with a smile I would never forget.

The music stopped and I stepped back to bow to Liz, and she appropriately curtsied to me. A round of applause was directed by most toward the band, whose members bowed to their audience. I took Liz's hand, and we walked near the windows to watch the next dance and catch our breath.

The music started for another "Quadrille Dance", and I checked the dance card. "You know that a polka follows this 'Quadrille Dance', and Mr. Spitzer is on your card. We don't want to keep him waiting," I said with a smidgen of sarcasm.

"You have no reason to be jealous of Mr. Spitzer. He is a good dancer as you are also, Karl. I look forward to the last dance with you," Liz said as I pondered what the phrase "last dance" meant. Would we ever dance again? When, and where?

My thoughts returned to the moment as the music for "The Quadrille Dance" ended and Mr. Spitzer approached Liz, took her hand, and proceeded to dance the polka with her. I checked my dance card and noticed there was a "Les Lanciers" dance next followed by the last dance of the evening, our waltz.

Mr. Spitzer continued to impress with his skills, but I sensed from looking around the room that we were all a little tired and were ready for a slow waltz to end a perfect evening. The polka ended and Mr. Spitzer was most polite and kind to Liz. As some people had left for the evening there were a few chairs available near the windows, and I suggested Mr. Spitzer join us for conversation.

He respectfully declined and said he was finished dancing for the evening. Liz thanked him for the dances, and he left as we sat and enjoyed watching fewer "Les Lanciers" participants than before but nonetheless surprisingly enthusiastic for so late in the evening.

"I've had a wonderful time this evening with you, Liz. I will not long forget the fun we had, but also how beautiful you look and the glow of your smile," I said as Liz blushed a little and looked shyly down at her shoes.

"I tried not to imagine how much fun a ball dance like this would be, as we are supposed to keep a certain professional distance with the patrons. Fortunately, Herr Strand knows me well enough to trust my judgement. His patient teaching, understanding, guidance and most importantly trust have helped me become a better person and therefore a better employee. I am now further indebted to him for letting me take time to be with you and participate in this ball," she said as a cool breeze came in through the windows behind us and I placed my arm gently around her shoulders.

"I am also grateful to Herr Strand. If I have the opportunity, I will let him know," I said, as we held hands and enjoyed the "Les Lanciers" dance finish. Despite being late in the evening I did not notice a single missed step. We stood and assumed the proper position again as the band leader announced a slow waltz would be the final dance of the evening. The music began as we continued to enjoy our time together.

"I will miss you," she said softly as we moved around the ballroom floor. Tears began to well in her eyes and I told her I would miss her also. I decided I had to try again to encourage her to visit me.

"Please seriously consider visiting me in New York. I would love to have you meet my friends and show you the city," I said with absolute sincerity.

"Your friends would consider me a country girl who lacks sophistication, I'm sure," Liz said as I reassured her, they would not.

"Some people in New York confuse mean-spirited judgement with sophistication. I do not associate with those people. My friends would find you as delightful and uncomplicated as do I," I assured Liz.

"By uncomplicated, do you mean unsophisticated?" she asked.

"No. I mean that your daily surroundings and requirements here in the country are different from mine in the city. Life seems simpler here, less crowded, and therefore less hectic. I love your charm and connection with the natural surroundings. Most people in New York could not point North or know where or even how their food is grown," I said with confidence.

The music for the waltz ended and everyone stood, turned toward the bandstand, and applauded the band members for their fine performance. The band members all stood and took a bow, and some of Liz's girls came in and started to clean the refreshment table as a signal it was time to leave.

The Bath

As we left the ballroom together, I mentioned I would like to take a bath to sooth my aching body after dancing.

"Would it be too late to get water for my bath?" I asked hoping Liz could help but also concerned she did not upset anyone by doing something out of ordinary.

"I can let my girls know and they will bring up the water. Not a problem," she said with enough confidence that led me to believe it was not an unreasonable request so late in the evening. Liz returned to the ballroom and talked with a couple of her girls who were cleaning up after the dance. They nodded approvingly and she returned to me in the hall. We walked together upstairs as she explained the procedure.

"The girls bring a large bucket of water from the kitchen up a dumbwaiter at the end of the hall. We have a cart in the closet we use to wheel the water into the room and fill the tank above the tub and add water to the tub also. Gas heats up the tank and when it is hot, we open a spigot and add the hot tank water to the bath," she explained as I opened my room with the key.

When we entered the room, I took off my shoes and placed my jacket on the bed. Liz lit the candles in the candelabra, then proceeded to pull down the portable tub from the wall and show me the tank and heating system. A moment later I answered a knock on my door and opened to find two girls pulling a cart with a water bucket as Liz had described. They helped pour water from the bucket into the heating tank and placed towels on the dresser. Liz thanked the girls as they left, then closed the door and lit the gas to heat up the tank water. I removed my tie and placed it next to my jacket on the bed.

"I believe I can handle the rest myself. How long does it take to heat up the water?" I said as I turned around to see Liz remove her dress. More surprised than aroused, I stumbled for words as she stood almost naked in front of me.

"I can stay and help. Why don't you get ready?" she asked with a smile.

I removed my clothes, walked over to her, and pulled her close to me. Her ample breasts pressed against my chest, and we kissed passionately. All week I had imagined making love to her but was not sure how our relationship would progress. This was a surprise. A wonderful surprise.

A steam release valve on the tank made a noise and Liz said it was time for my bath. She turned off the gas, released a lever and hot water poured through a steel tube into the bathtub. I got into the tub and kissed Liz as she knelt next to me. I fondled her breasts as she reached into the tub with a towel and finished me. Relaxed and pleased the way the evening ended, I sank into the warm water as Liz rubbed my chest hair and offered to scrub my back.

"You surprised me. A most pleasant surprise, however," I said as she gently washed my back.

"I love you, Karl, and I will miss you very much," she said sadly as she rested her head on my shoulder.

"I could not have imagined my visit here, my vacation, would introduce me to someone like you. That I would fall in love. Tomorrow I must leave and that…" I said as I sighed. As I tried to continue, she placed her finger to my lips. I put my head back and enjoyed the moment.

Tired from the evening and with the bath water getting cooler I kissed her gently as she helped me out of the tub and handed me a towel. She noticed the knife wrapped in the oily towel on the chest of drawers.

"Is this your knife?" she asked as I dried myself and we both got dressed.

"Yes. I like it but really have no practical purpose for it. Not like Stu," letting her know I was quite impressed with the skills he possessed. She picked up and smelled the pine pillow.

"Can you stay a while longer?" I asked as I moved my jacket and tie off the bed. "I just want to hug you, be with you a while longer," I said, as I sat on the bed and encouraged her to sit by me.

"I can stay. But I cannot spend the evening," she said as she sat next to me, and we hugged.

"I understand. Just lie with me here a while," I offered, and she agreed. We snuggled on the bed side-by-side.

A rush overcame me, and I felt like I was always supposed to be there, with her, in that room, at that time. I felt we were part of a plan, a large plan that included us and all that happened was meant to be. As we lay there, quietly, holding each other I asked, "Do you believe in coincidence. I mean, do you think we were meant to be together?" I asked as a cool breeze entered the room.

"I don't know. I believe we are lucky. My parents have always been a good example of a loving couple. I have an aunt and a few uncles who never got married. Most seem content alone. But I believe some of my uncles would have liked to get married and have a family. It just never happened for them," she said as we snuggled closer.

"I believe a life alone would be difficult. I have never come close to getting married, however," I said as I watched her face for a reaction.

"Do you think we would make a good couple. I mean, would we learn to hate our differences, would you tire of me?" an allusion to us as a married couple Liz asked as a tear formed in her eye.

"I would not tire of you and believe our differences would make us a respectable couple. There would be many different subjects on which we could expound and hopefully entertain our relatives and friends," I said as she gave me a long hug.

"I love the idea of us being together into old age. Last night I spent imagining being together if God would allow us," she said as she began to get up off the bed and put on her shoes. A feeling of sadness that we would not be able to spend another day together began to overwhelm me. Each minute now was one more minute toward my departure the next day. I stood and hugged and kissed her and we said good night. It was late by now and she noted she must work the next day.

"I want to say goodbye when you take the train tomorrow. When are you leaving?" she asked as I walked her quietly down the hall to the stairwell.

"I leave a little after 10:00 AM. I would love to say goodbye then. Do you think you could be there?" I asked.

"I will be there," she said with a slightly sad voice. We kissed at the top of the stairs, and I noticed she was still wearing the necklace I gave her as she walked down and disappeared into the evening. I walked back to my room with thoughts of us marrying in Central Park with our friends and family. I imagined her sister's goats eating the floral arrangements and us taking a lavish white horse carriage to the newly opened Waldorf Astoria Hotel.

As I entered my room it seemed empty and silent, without her energy and love. Would my life be like this room without her? I got undressed and blew out the candles. Thoughts of packing my things to be ready in the morning quickly faded as I collapsed into my bed from exhaustion. The bed still smelled like her lilac perfume.

The morning bells in the hall woke me from my deep slumber and I sat up unnerved and convinced I had missed my train. After the morning fog lifted from my thoughts and I realized I was fine, I lay back down and reviewed my plans for my morning. A cool breeze filtered through my room's curtains, and I hesitated to leave the warmth of my bed for the cold mist on the portico. I fell back to sleep and was awakened by the brightness in my room.

Convinced food might be a difficult commodity to obtain as my day progressed, I checked my watch and decided I had ample time to pack after breakfast. The line for breakfast was long at the base of the stairs, and I quietly shuffled in with a group as we entered the dining room.

"Looking forward to some coffee?" a nice-looking young man asked as we sat together at a table. The evening must have taken a toll and left its mark on my tired face.

"I'm a little tired from dancing last evening. Hopefully I don't look too bad," I asked as a waiter poured our coffee.

"Oh no, you look fine. I was just looking for conversation. I'm Sam and this is Olivia," he said as he introduced himself and his wife seated next to him.

"Were you also at the ball last night?" I asked, encouraged by our mutually shared interest in intriguing banter.

"No, we plan to attend the ball this Friday. We were at the bar last night and heard the band. The beautiful music that drifted through the hotel was accompanied by the shifting of feet and creaking of the ballroom floor right above us. Did you have a good time?" he asked as the waiters began to distribute the morning meal.

"We had a wonderful time. Liz, my consort, and I enjoyed dancing and I agree the Smiths Cornet Band were a fine and very capable ensemble. They switched easily in and out of different time and key signatures without missing a note," I said as I decided to wait for the meat dishes to be served. I thought meat may allow me to feel less hungry later during my long travel back to New York City. But I also knew there would be food choices on the ship from Kingston to New York.

My preoccupation with my potential future lack of access to food was a distraction and a way to hopefully forget, however momentarily, that I would no longer be with my Liz.

"You must be a musician to notice such nuances in the band's performance," Sam noted as I returned my attention back to the moment.

"I took piano lessons for years," I said as more food arrived at our table, and I placed a steak and a scoop of corned beef hash on my plate. "The lessons were annoying and time consuming. I would rather have been playing with my friends. But now I play an hour a day and find it relaxing and rewarding," I continued as poached eggs and bacon were being passed.

To not be perceived as rude I attempted to have a conversation with the elderly woman to my right. She gave me a look that was colder than the ice in the kitchen cooler, so I refrained from furthering that endeavor.

Sam's wife Olivia had not entered the conversation and was very quiet. She was slim and beautiful, and together they were an attractive couple. I returned my attention to my younger acquaintances and always curious, I inquired of Sam's occupation.

"I work for a company that manufactures fire prevention equipment of all kinds, big and small. Buckets, pumps, hoses…our company also manufactures the new glass hand grenade fire extinguishers," he said as I asked the waiter for more coffee. "After a few years with the International Fire Equipment Company I transferred from manufacturing to testing the equipment.

Olivia thinks it is a dangerous job, but it is all well controlled. We construct test buildings on our company property and set fire to them to ensure the quality of our products," he said proudly.

I thanked our waiter for his continued attentiveness, then remarked, "My office and other offices I visit have installed fire extinguisher box kits which contain the newer glass grenades. I must believe you receive satisfaction knowing your company's products help save lives," as I let him know my occupation as an accountant had no such esteem.

"The management of our company often discuss and research the likelihood of someone remembering to open the box and throw a hand grenade extinguisher at a fire during such a traumatic calamity. We encourage and offer training when the extinguisher boxes are installed. Even infrequent use of our products saves lives, and it is reassuring when we receive letters from survivors," he said proudly as he concurred my observation.

Feeling comfortable with my new acquaintances I inquired what activities they pursue for pleasure.

"Olivia participates in horse jumping competitions. We also love to go to music shows and plays," he said as we finished our meal and people began leaving the dining room. I thanked him for his time and that I appreciated our conversation. Olivia gave me a quiet nod goodbye as she took Sam's arm, and we all left the dining room bidding each other a fine day.

Goodbye

Looking at my watch I realized I had time to say goodbye to Madelyn in the office. The fragrant boughs of pine that hung in the hallway was soon overpowered by the smell of stale beer as I passed the bar door. Noticing that the kitchen door was open, I stepped in to thank them for their fine food preparations. The kitchen staff was, as always, busy scraping plates and dishes into garbage bins, sweeping, and mopping the floor.

Kris was busy supervising but took the time to shake my hand and thank me for my compliment. His large hand was rough and a little greasy, and his smile and appreciation was genuine. I walked further down the hall and looked in the office to see that Madelyn was at her desk and did not appear too busy. I entered and she greeted me with a smile.

"Last day, huh. Liz sure is going to miss you. You make a nice pair," she offered, and I thanked her for her compliment.

"You have made it clear you know Liz and how she feels about me. I would appreciate it if you would answer another question. Has she mentioned visiting me in New York City? She has eluded the subject when I tried to discuss," I asked, hoping Maddy could give me some insight into Liz's thoughts.

"Liz has mentioned wanting to visit you. Her constraints are money and time, both in short supply. She would never take money from you, no matter how well intentioned," Maddy said as Sebastian leaned on my leg with his good front leg and wagged his tail for attention.

"I will miss you, *kleiner Hund,*" I said as I bent down and gently scratched his back. "Is Herr Strand available? I would like to thank him for his hospitality and my fine experience at his hotel," I queried.

"He left early this morning for the valley. He had a meeting with local businessmen and dignitaries at the Presbyterian Church in Catskill. I'm sorry to let you know he won't be back until this evening," Maddy said as she noticed new arrivals coming in the back entrance.

"I will bother you no more. Please let Herr Strand know he exceeded his fine reputation as host of this delightful edifice and be sure to give Liz my address. Thank you for all your help and I appreciated your honesty. I wish you well and hope to see you again," I said to Maddy as I left the office.

She said it was fine to leave my key in my room and informed me that Greg would be out near the back of the hotel in about thirty minutes to take me to Otis Summit. She also wished me well as she returned to her work. I checked my watch again, and it was over an hour until my train left Otis Summit so I walked to the portico and sat where I could appreciate the view one last time.

A server asked if I would like something to drink and I asked for lemonade. A warm breeze swept the portico as I watched clouds move across the valley below. He returned with my drink, I tipped him well, and he thanked me twice for my generosity.

The beauty of the view made me wonder why I had not spent more time on the porch, but I reminded myself that I did experience much of the surrounding area and visited two other hotels. I finished my drink and returned to my room, which seemed lifeless and duller than before. I packed as well as I could, and as I placed my key on the dresser, I noticed my knife. Certain I would have forgotten the knife, I checked to be sure I remembered to pack the pine pillow. Despite the grimy nature of the clothes in my suitcase, the pine pillow provided a pleasant fragrance to my wardrobe.

Several patrons walked past and greeted me with smiles and nods as I descended the stairs and walked down the hall, out of the hotel and sat by a table under a tree near the back entrance.

Familiar with the routine, I nonetheless continued my interested observation of men unloading ox and horse carts with meat, vegetables, ice, and other items as I waited for Greg to arrive.

Thick clouds blocked the sun, and it looked like it might rain. Several of Liz's girls guided small children away from the goats which were tied near the southern corner of the hotel, slowly pulling up and chewing grass clumps while occasionally letting out a loud bleat.

A few men from the kitchen joined other workers near me to smoke and grumble about everything, but mostly about the bad weather they were sure was coming soon. A buckboard pulled up to the hotel and I saw Greg held the reins. Dust kicked up as he jumped off the front and grabbed a large, heavy bag from the back of the wagon and carried it into the hotel.

To ensure he wouldn't leave without me, I placed my suitcase where the bag had been and waited patiently by the wagon for Greg to return. He returned within minutes and acknowledged my presence with a nod and a polite hello.

"Good to see you again, Greg. I would appreciate a ride to Otis Summit as I am leaving today," I said as he sat in the front of the buckboard and grabbed the reins.

"Any more luggage?" Greg asked as he winked and smiled at one of Liz's girls as she walked near the wagon.

"This is all I brought. We can leave whenever you are ready," I said as I looked up and noticed the sky had darkened further and became increasingly concerned about the weather.

"Probly' won't rain for another hour or so," Greg said with effortless confidence. He continued, "We'll wait a few minutes for anyone else."

"I'm curious - what was in the bag you delivered?" I inquired as we had a few moments.

"My Aunt Margaret's summer squash. Green, yellow, green with stripes…she grows the sweetest squash in Greene County," he said proudly. After a few minutes Greg surmised we were the only passengers on this brief trip, so with a quick "HE-YAA" and a tug of the reins we quickly rolled away from the hotel. As we reached the edge of the woods and the trail down to the Otis Summit Station, I turned to view the hotel one final time.

My vacation was pleasurable beyond my finest expectations, and I assured myself I would return when possible. Greg tipped his hat politely to a few patrons we passed on the road which sloped down through the patch of woods toward the station. Ruts in the road shook the old buckboard wagon vigorously and I wondered if we might lose a wheel during our short excursion.

The road leveled off as we left the woods and reached the station. The clouds appeared more menacing as I tipped Greg and told him I enjoyed our times together. Tall grass on a hill near the station whipped in unison from the wind coming up the valley as I grabbed my bag and proceeded up the stairs.

I walked to the waiting area near the ticket office, sat on a bench and noticed there were two passenger railcars at the station, both red with grey roofs. At the same moment I verified my ticket was in my shirt pocket I felt a soft touch on my shoulder. It was Liz! I stood and we hugged for several moments.

"I don't have much time and must get back to my duties. Please promise to write," she said as she held back tears.

"Of course. I'll write often and look forward to your letters. Maddy has my address," I said as we held hands on the small porch overlooking my waiting train on the tracks below us. The train engine occasionally spewed out a loud jet of steam as we stared at each other and searched for the words which would convey our mutual grief over my departure and our separation.

At that moment the ticket booth operator stepped out on the porch and announced they would be boarding the train now. As other passengers gathered their luggage, we hugged one last time.

"I love you Liz and will miss you so much my heart will ache," I said sincerely. She gently grabbed my shoulders as she placed her head on my chest and softly sobbed.

"I love you too Karl," she said as she lifted her head and kissed me. We gently parted as I picked up my luggage and said, "Goodbye Liz," as I stared deeply into her green eyes through the mist of my own tears.

"Goodbye Karl," she said and followed me down the steps to the train platform. We kissed one last time and held hands for a moment. I turned and entered the train as she stepped back onto the platform and waved goodbye. She blew me a kiss and I watched her walk away as far as my window would allow. I fought back tears and stared in the distance, contemplating my life without her.

The Kaaterskill Railroad

The Kaaterskill Railroad Station

"Tickets please," barked the Kaaterskill Railroad conductor, which shook me from my self-pity. Short and elderly with a white beard and a brown suit he moved quickly for his age, and as he punched my ticket I asked when we would be leaving.

"Momentarily," he said as he moved down the rail car. The smell of cigarettes heralded the arrival of my anticipated travel companion Mr. Schroeder.

"Good to see you again Harold," I said as I welcomed his company and the diversion from my dismal disposition.

"I saw you with her at the platform and kept my distance as I didn't want to intrude. You both fell hard for each other, huh?" he said as he took a seat next to me on the narrow train. His instincts to keep his physical distance obviously didn't apply to personal discussions of a sensitive nature. Nonetheless, I addressed his inquiry.

"Yes, we are in love. It seems illogical, at first thought. Even though we are from different backgrounds and had different experiences, it felt as if we've known each other a long time," I expounded, feeling no boundaries to my expressions as we would probably never meet again. My curiosity preceded a desire to also ask questions of a personal nature.

"Are you married?" I felt emboldened to inquire.

"Yes, she is a wonderful woman. She accepts my long trips and frequent failures in my business. Insurance sales is difficult. After the 'Panic of 1884' many businesses and people no longer trusted the insurance companies. Now, it's been eight years since then, but the lingering mistrust remains. My work is rewarding when I can help a business recover from a calamity. Oh, before I forget, would you please pass my business cards to businesses in New York City you think could benefit from our services?" he said as he thrust a pile of his cards near my hand.

"Of course," I said as I placed the cards in my jacket pocket. "Is there any specialty business your company tends to insure?" I asked.

"We insure businesses of many types. We recently paid for the reconstruction of a power plant that caught fire in Mechanicville," he offered as proof of his company's integrity.

"Interesting. Do you insure homes also?" I further inquired, as I realized our conversation continued to be a gratifying diversion from my previous melancholy mood.

"Of course," Harold said as the train began to slowly move toward the lakes.

Although the entire railcar was encircled in windows, I strained to observe the places with which I had become familiar. We passed the beach and boathouse, and a little "toot!" of the train signaled we were going to pick up speed and climb the hill on the other side of the lakes.

Our conductor entered our train car and sat down the moment we passed between the lakes. Evidently, his experience affirmed the knowledge that he would not get secure footing while this narrow-gauge train climbed the hill. The train spewed steam as we passed through heavy woods, and it became noticeably darker and began to rain. Our railcar swayed back and forth as we barely missed branches on both sides of the train.

"Next stop Laurel House and Kaaterskill Falls," our conductor announced as we came to a halt. A few people entered the railcar behind our car and a few passengers disembarked into the miserable-looking weather. This process continued as we made several brief stops at places named Sunset View, The Antlers Hotel, Haines Corners, and Clum Road.

As we crossed a trestle spanning a small stream in Haines Corners, I noticed nearby several workmen roofing a beautiful house under final construction while an older gentleman sat on the porch smoking a pipe. The housing in the Catskills was a variety of mixed styles and worth, with basic boarding houses and simple dwellings near elegant residences, beautiful manors, and large hotels.

The Tannersville Railroad Station

"Next stop Tannersville," declared our conductor as he walked through our railcar and into the other.

"Do you know which steamship you will take to New York?" asked Harold, who had been quiet for so long I had almost forgotten he was next to me. "I have a schedule if you'd like to look at it," offered Harold as he fished a crumpled schedule from his jacket. I told him I appreciated the offer and asked if he remembered when we were scheduled to arrive in Kingston Point.

"I think we are scheduled to arrive in Kingston around 1:00 PM. Looks like the *New York* leaves at 2:20 PM from Kingston Point. It is a grand ship. The sister ship to the *Albany*," he said as I perused the wrinkled paper.

"I was a passenger on the *Albany* from New York to Catskill. You must know the ships well as you travel for your business," I offered to continue our discussion.

"Yes, living in Poughkeepsie I use the Hudson for my main transportation. Catskill, Hudson, Albany, Troy…I have business clients in many cities along the river," Harold continued.

"I have visited Albany but have never been to Troy. A veterinarian I met at the hotel told me the hills are very steep," I said as we entered the Tannersville Railroad Station.

Numerous people waited on the station platform to board the destinations serviced by this location. The men mostly wore suits in brown and grey colors, but the crowded station was a rainbow of women and girls in colorful dresses and little boys outfitted in jackets, knickers, and boots. Round hats shaded their faces as several passengers boarded our train.

"Next stop Kaaterskill Junction. Those going to Hunter get off at Kaaterskill Junction. Those passengers going to Phoenicia stay on board," spouted our conductor as the train started to move.

"I have plenty of business opportunities along the Hudson, but winter weather makes it difficult to travel. Sometimes I wish we lived where it is warmer. I know my wife would like that," Harold said wistfully as we agreed that New York State winters can be brutal. I mentioned to Harold I had observed the landscape change from industry to farming as I traveled further upstate, and how much respect I had for those who work the land.

"I have insured a few farms. Farming is a tough life. The growing season is short around here and sometimes a large rainstorm can wash away an entire crop planting. Other seasons are dry, or pestilence or many other terrible occurrences can ruin a farm in just one year," Harold said as the train stopped.

The Stony Clove and Catskill Mountain Railroad

Kaaterskill Junction

"Kaaterskill Junction. All passengers going to Hunter get off here. Passengers going to Phoenicia stay on board," repeated our reliable conductor as he also disembarked at the station. I felt a slight jolt and noticed our railcar was added to the rear of another car.

"Welcome to the Stony Clove and Catskill Mountain Railroad. We will depart soon. Next stop Edgewood," stated our new conductor as he passed through our railcar. He was tall with a thick mustache and wore a white shirt, a dark grey suit, and a matching grey hat embroidered with the railroad logo. The train jerked slightly again as we began to move out of the station.

I noticed a little girl seated next to her mother was dressed very well and carried a sun umbrella. The mother encouraged her child to count the number of people in our car, then count the number of windows and so on. An older gentleman was reading the paper with his legs crossed. A few couples, old and young, filled out the rest of our railcar passengers. We left the wooded area that surrounded the Kaaterskill Junction Station and began a descent that never seemed to end. I wondered how the train could possibly brake at stations with the tracks so steep.

"The Ulster and Delaware train from Phoenicia to Kingston is much more stable since it is standard width. These narrow-gauge trains in the mountains always seem to be ready to fly off these mountain passes," Harold said as our train swerved around rock outcrops, over small trestle bridges and began to rock back and forth. Referred to as a "clove" or "notch", the train entered a dark, steep downward cut between the mountains.

The Stony Clove

So vertical was the topography that there were no streets or dwellings in the clove forest, and I admit I felt strange as we passed through. Trees were perched growing out of a thin layer of soil over angled rocks and huge boulders. What sunlight reached the notch seemed little enough to sustain any plant life whatsoever.

Our train leveled off and the wheels screeched as we stopped at the smallest train station I had ever seen. One person left the train and as we started again, we quickly picked up speed and continued down the notch. I yawned to adjust my ears to the changing pressure. A sign for the "Fenwick Mill Sawmill" was prominent as we left the small town of Edgewood.

Harold had been quiet for a while, and I noticed the gentle rocking of the railcar had lulled him to sleep. We passed a few more sawmills after a brief stop at Lanesville Station, and a sign for the "Chichester Furniture Factory" greeted us before the Chichester Station stop.

"Next stop Phoenicia. All passengers will be directed to walk along the Phoenicia Station platform while the gauge is switched. You may leave your belongings in your railcar. The Stony Clove and Catskill Mountain Railroad thanks you for your business," said our conductor as sunlight finally entered our windows as we left the clove. We crossed a river and began to pass streets and houses again as the train leveled off and slowed.

The Stony Clove

The Ulster and Delaware Railroad

The Phoenicia Railroad Station

The Phoenicia Station railroad yard was quite large, with several Ulster and Delaware engines and railcars distributed on multiple parallel tracks. Our train stopped at a platform, and we were directed where to walk to enter our railcar after the switch was completed. Harold immediately availed himself of the opportunity for a smoke as we slowly walked along the covered platform.

"You may want to watch the process," Harold said as he took a long drag on his cigarette. "It is interesting to watch. Our train car gets moved onto another set of larger wheels so we can continue with a regular gauge train," he said with fascinated fervor. I took his advice and attempted to comprehend the process I observed. Men directed horses attached to a pole, and cables were used to drag each railcar over a section of track that was depressed in the ground.

As the car passed over the depression, beams of wood on wider wheels lifted the railcar off the pins as the smaller railcar wheels rolled into the depression between the tracks. As the car moved forward the larger wheels were inserted under the pins and the car was then positioned on the wider tracks.

I am not sure I understood the entire process, but "Ramsey's Car Transfer Apparatus" was proudly painted on a station building and obviously was a successful invention. In less than an hour several cars were switched, we re-entered our railcar and were on our way to Kingston.

"Welcome to the Ulster and Delaware Railroad. Next stop Mt. Pleasant," said our new young conductor who wore a deep blue colored suit, a white shirt, and a black hat. Our ride was now steadier, smoother, and less tumultuous than our previous smaller gauge train as Harold had noted.

"The park in Kingston looked interesting. Have you visited before?" I asked as Harold checked how many cigarettes he had left in his jacket pocket.

"I take my wife and children to Kingston Point Park a few times a summer. A brief ride across the Hudson and we're there. The children like to play at the beach, and we sometimes rent a canoe and paddle around the lagoon. We enjoy the park at Kingston," Harold said as we left the Phoenicia Station.

"I read in the papers that the Ulster and Delaware Railroad may run a full-sized gauge train all the way to Hunter," Harold offered as I noticed the little girl in our car asleep in her mother's lap.

"With the Stony Clove Notch so steep it must have been very difficult working conditions to install the existing tracks. I do not envy those workers," I said as Harold shook his head in agreement.

"Several Italians I've met who worked on the Stony Clove Railroad hated the conditions. Rocks, trees, roots, mud, insects, and often intolerable heat. And yet they complained our rivers were too cold for baths," Harold said as he chuckled at the thought.

Although our train continued to descend, the descent was much more gradual than our trip through the clove. Cross streets, houses and businesses were becoming more common as we continued to leave the Great Wall of Manitou and move closer to the Hudson.

Our train stopped briefly at the Mt. Pleasant Station where a girl on a bicycle waved, and several horse carriages awaited passengers who got off at the Cold Brook Station. Vendors were selling vegetables on crates near the station platform, and I observed side tracks across from the Boiceville Station that led to a structure used for loading freight railcars.

We crossed a river on a wooden trestle bridge and passed by the houses, blacksmith shop, wagon shop, and Boiceville Inn that comprised the Boiceville hamlet. Between the Shokan Station and Brodhead's Bridge Station we passed a tannery and began to level off as we left the mountains behind us. Thick forests were now replaced by the familiar brown and green acres of farmland separated by a few trees in hedgerows.

Another sawmill near Brown's Station named MacArthur Brothers Winston & Company allowed me to reasonably conclude that these industries took advantage of the thick forests nearby and the transportation opportunities such as the trains and rivers.

"The furniture businesses make sense. The trees, the water power and the available transportation options must be ideal for that industry," I said as I shared my thoughts with Harold, who was also gazing out the window.

"Furniture businesses are tough to insure. The wood, sawdust, wood preservatives…they can catch fire from a spark and burn to the ground," Harold said. Unfortunately, because of my profession as an accountant I tended to calculate everything by its monetary value. Conversely, Harold tended to evaluate the assets and liabilities of a particular business. I pondered the possibly that our professions blurred the vision we have of something and could also obscure its true meaning or value.

To continue our conversation about businesses in the area I asked Harold what other industries were common for him to insure.

"Well, there's quite a variety. We have brick kilns, mining, quarries and stone shipping yards, tourism, farming. The tanning industry has died out. Anyway, not too long until we are in Kingston," he said as our train meandered through fields of grain, corn, and other crops.

An occasional field of wildflowers would share their delightful scent through our windows. Industries were becoming more frequent as we stopped briefly at the Olive Branch, West Hurley, and Stony Hollow stations. Small fishing boats and sailboats dotted the meandering river we followed as we entered Kingston.

Kingston Point Park

Kingston Point Park

"Kingston Union Station next, with connections to the West Shore Railroad," expounded our conductor as I momentarily thought we were at the end of our trip. After I took a quick look out the window, I could see we were at a large station but were not yet at Kingston Point.

"Next stop Rondout. We arrive in Kingston Point in ten minutes," announced our conductor as he steadied himself walking through our car. Several manufacturing businesses lined the tracks as we entered the Rondout Station. Grey, foul smoke enveloped our railcar from the local industry, and I longed to smell wildflowers again.

Slowly we pulled into our destination, and I began to appreciate the size and attributes of Kingston Point Park indiscernible by my obstructed view from the ship days before. People leisurely paddled canoes around a small gazebo in the middle of the lagoon that was connected by a foot bridge to the plentiful walking trails that abounded in the park. Occasional small sun-shaded stands with benches dotted the park, and every building was white with a steep-pitched dark red roof.

As I checked my watch our train slowed next to a long, covered train platform parallel to the river between the pavilion and the lagoon. I noted that I had more than an hour to walk the park trails and get refreshments before the steamship *New York* would arrive.

The two-story pavilion near the Hudson water's edge was quite well attended and I observed signs for refreshments at "Bachner's Tavern" on the first floor. Signs for "Clam Chowder", "Ice Cream" and "Souvenirs" were prominent on a stand near the pavilion platform.

"Kingston Point Park. Steamship and trolley service is available from here. The Ulster and Delaware Railroad thanks you for your patronage," said our conductor as our train came to a full stop parallel to a narrowly covered section of the large wooden dock.

Benches on one side of the dock separated our train tracks from the Hudson River shore where the steamships arrived. As we departed the train, a porter asked my destination and carried my suitcase to a storage area near the dock where a ticket attendant asked my name, which ship I would be boarding, and my destination.

I obliged his requests, and after I paid for my ticket, he marked my suitcase with tags and noted, "The *New York*. She's a fine ship. It will arrive and board in about an hour." I tipped both the porter and the attendant and decided to walk around the park before I sought nourishment. Our train spent little time at Kingston Point Park Station, as it gave a quick "toot!" of the whistle and a ring of the bell when it pulled out only minutes after arriving.

Thankfully, the grey clouds in the mountains that had threatened rain earlier in the day had dissipated. Yellow trolley cars waited at a small but busy trolley station on a hill a short distance from the pavilion. White benches were dispersed along the pathways in the park, and there were as many people sitting and observing as were walking in the midday sun. Along the Hudson water's edge were many more places for repose and to appreciate the magnificent views of the river and passing ships.

The pathways were crowded with debonaire women in long dresses and hats, girls in knee-high dresses, men in suits and caps, and boys equally dapper in jackets and knickers. No one seemed in a hurry, and I welcomed the relaxed atmosphere. A merry-go-round with wooden carved and painted horses held the attention of several spectators as excited children tried desperately to grab the brass ring and win another ride.

I continued to walk the park paths and noticed the gazebo in the middle of the lagoon had music stands for a band. Frequent large circles of well-manicured flowers divided the pathways and added color and splendor to the area. Satisfied I had perused the park sufficiently to satisfy my curiosity I walked back toward Bachner's Tavern where I hoped to have a beer with lunch.

To my surprise a woman began yelling something near me and then yelled clearly, "My little girl! My little Ruby is missing!" she kept repeating as she pushed frantically through the crowd looking in every direction. Shaken from my relaxed mood and desperate to help her, I fortunately heard someone loudly say there was a girl alone by the merry-go-round.

I notified the frantic mother who ran over and picked up her daughter, who obviously was fascinated by the movement and music enough to leave her family. There was a collective sigh of relief from the people in my immediate vicinity, and anxious spectators in the crowd who were aware of the crisis returned to their conversations and strolling. As I watched the mother return her daughter to her two sisters and father, I was gratified in the small part I played helping the family reunite. I also determined a beer was now not a want but a need, and I proceeded to the order counter for Bachner's Tavern and paid for my desired beer and a bratwurst.

Although grey clouds were again spoiling the sunshine it appeared rain would not disturb my day in the park. Nonetheless, I carried my refreshments upstairs and sought a table under the shade and protection of the pavilion. Open on all sides, the cool breeze from the Hudson smelled like rain.

With views of the river on one side and the beautiful park on the other it was difficult to decide where to sit. I chose a table near the park as I determined there would be plentiful river views while aboard the *New York*. Content with my sausage and beer, I observed several people sitting in the benches that faced and lined the lattice patterned railing on the park side of the pavilion. Couples walked close together through trails that twisted around a small grove of trees on a hill near the main trails.

Experienced men rowed boats around the gazebo bandstand in the lagoon, and I was reminded of my amateurish failed attempt in North Lake at that endeavor. Fortunately, my audience was much smaller and less attentive. I left the pavilion and walked toward the souvenir stand.

Having checked my watch, I decided to wait on the dock for my ship, scheduled to arrive in twenty minutes. After purchasing my cigars at the souvenir stand near the pavilion, a hint of sunlight reflected off jewelry on the stand. I decided to also purchase the small silver bracelet with an embossed 'Hudson River Day Line' steamship on a silver heart charm with a small key, suspended on a twisted silver chain. I hoped to deliver the gift to Liz in person.

Hudson River Day Line souvenir bracelet

A bench in the shade on the large dock near the south side of the pavilion provided an ideal place where I could observe and enjoy a cigar. Pleased with my selected location, I proceeded to enjoy my smoke as porters in their black suits, caps and suspenders wandered near the storage area in anticipation of loading the ship.

Some of them were also smoking, and although I could not hear what they were saying I could see by their smiles and camaraderie that they were enjoying each other's company. Assured I could not possibly miss my ship, I relaxed as my thoughts returned to my time at the hotel and, of course, Liz. I wondered how long it would be until I received a letter from her.

Going Home

The steamship *New York* of the Hudson River Day Line
docked at Kingston Point

More people and employees were filling the dock, and as I finished my cigar, I heard a ship's whistle in the distance. Soon the large, white steamship *New York* slowly pulled up to the dock. Hudson River Day Line employees hurried to tie off the thick mooring ropes to the dock anchors tossed by deckhands from the ship. When the waves from the ship had adequately subsided two gangplanks were extended to the dock, one for the passengers and the other for loading suitcases, rectangular trunks, and other cargo.

I joined the stream of passengers and had my ticket punched as I boarded. The porters transported trunks of various sizes in two lengthy, continuous lines with one hand on the trunk in front of them and the other hand holding the handle of the trunk behind them. So fascinated watching the procession I almost bumped into the woman in front of me.

"I didn't see you in the park," said a man to my right as I walked near the railing of the ship.

"Harold, you surprised me," I said slightly startled as we both found a spot to lean on the railing and watched the ship load.

"It was crowded. Did you hear the woman who couldn't find her child?" I asked to rekindle another of our many conversations.

"No, I missed that. I am always concerned about my children near water," he said as he lit a cigarette. "Was the child OK?" he asked, concerned, as he exhaled smoke into the breeze.

"Yes. It was only a minute. But I'm sure it seemed longer to the family," I said, assured that being a father, Harold knew better the fears that must accompany such a situation.

A loud steam whistle blasted as the loading gang planks and mooring ropes were removed. Another loud "toot!" of the whistle and the grand steamship *New York* began moving away from the dock. The sign "Kingston Point Park" on the roof of the pavilion faded in the distance as we picked up speed.

"You were right. This ship is almost identical to the *Albany*. If I remember correctly, we have an hour until Poughkeepsie. Can I buy you a beer?" I asked as I knew I would probably not see him again and wished to show my appreciation for his friendship and conversations.

"Sure, I would enjoy that. Follow me," Harold said assuredly as we walked past the huge iron arm moving up and down powering us southbound. The sound of the steam engine faded as we walked up stairs to the second level and straight to a bar near a small band. Paintings on the walls, comfortable chairs and thick mahogany wood defined the room where three violinists performed with other musicians playing a trumpet, tuba, bass, and piano. I realized on my trip to the Catskills I never visited the second level of the steamship *Albany* and must have missed the band there.

We sat at a table where we could converse and still listen to the performance. A waitress was quick with our order and when she returned with our drinks I paid, tipped her, and asked her if there was a music program. Perusing the concert schedule she brought while we enjoyed the beers and music, I was impressed by the variety, diversity, and complexity of the musical selections. The mix of Rubinstein and Puccini with modern pieces would have challenged any professional musician.

Harold and I raised our beer mugs to each other as we relaxed to the fine music. It was then I then understood why I had never heard a band while walking the decks of the *Albany*. Even though we sat close, I strained to hear their musical performance over the noise of people talking and the constant "whoosh!" of the engine. A few patrons joined my enthusiastic applause after they finished a piece, and I personally received a thankful nod of appreciation my way from two of the musicians.

As we sipped the last of our beers, we stood up slowly and both stretched our backs as travel and different sleeping arrangements can often make anyone ache.

"The next trip to the Mountain House I'll take the Otis Elevating Railway up the mountain. I think my back still hurts from the carriage ride," Harold said as we walked to the port side and watched sailing ships move up the river as we headed south. While we leaned on the railing and enjoyed the view, Harold lit a cigarette and said thoughtfully, "The Lenape Indians called the Hudson '*Mahicantuck*', which means river that flows two ways. It's true, the Hudson River changes direction several times a day."

The steamship *New York* of the Hudson River Day Line

"Interesting. New York City is on the Hudson, and I did not know that. This vacation has been a pleasant respite from the frequent drudgery keeping my nose to paper tallying numbers all day. I appreciate you sharing your time with me the last few days. It has been a pleasure to get to know you, Harold," I said sincerely.

Harold said he also enjoyed my company as we watched two well-dressed women coyly turn their sun umbrellas as they promenaded by us on the deck. Despite the open-air breezes I could smell their perfume, and they looked at us and gave a brief smile as they passed. Returning our attention to the river, I asked about temptations while away from home.

The steamships *Albany* and *New York* of the Hudson River Day Line passing near the Poughkeepsie Bridge

"Oh, I must be careful. I don't mislead women to believe I'm available. I am very happy in my home," he said with a boyish smile. I heard our ship give another "toot!" as our ship passed the steamship *Albany* near the railroad trestle bridge close to Poughkeepsie. Harold snuffed out his cigarette and shook my hand.

"It has been a pleasure. You have my card. If I secured any business in New York, I would be deeply grateful. You know New York City is a tough market. I must get off now," he said rather quickly as we shook hands again. Our steamship slowed and docked at Poughkeepsie. A "Day Line" flag fluttered on a pole near buildings separated by a wide dirt road.

No park in sight, this was simply a place to dock. A few people transferred on the gangplank, and I watched Harold as he approached a carriage and hugged his wife and two children. I waved as our ship moved southward again but he never looked back. I imagined having children with Liz, and how wonderful a family we would make.

The contentment and satisfaction Harold exuded when he described his home life further convinced me it was a good life for a man. I remembered the abolitionist John Brown was quoted as saying, "A man can hardly get into difficulties too big to be surmounted if he has a firm foothold at home." I believed that to be true. Yet, questions began planting seeds of doubt in my mind. Was it just a summer romance? Would the further apart we spend douse the fire in our hearts? Should I plan to visit the mountain house again soon?

Hudson River Day Line Indian Point Park

Somehow, we needed to be together again. Not just to confirm our love but to determine our commitment and what we both wanted out of the relationship. The letter I would send Liz when I returned to New York was being formed in my head as I took a seat on a bench near the bow. Liz needed to know how much I loved her and how I believed we could have a life together.

Our ship took a wide turn as we passed mountains on both sides of the Hudson. The river was beginning to widen, and I continued to contemplate our future as we stopped at Newburgh. We passed Bannerman's Castle as the river narrowed and we stopped at West Point. The letter to Liz was written and rewritten many times in my head as I wandered the decks of the ship.

Knowing I had a few more hours until we arrived in New York I revisited the restaurant on the second level, sat down near the band and asked the server for a menu. Feeling alone, I now longed for the routine of my life in the city and sharing my northern adventure with friends. I wondered if I returned to my business and social acquaintances would my time with Liz seem like a dream and fade into memory?

"Can I take your order, sir," the waiter asked as I tried to concentrate on the moment. I ordered a Shepherd's Pie and a root beer as I continued to contemplate my future. Our future. We stopped at Bear Mountain and then Indian Point as I finished my second root beer and gave a generous applause for our band's performance.

After I paid and tipped my server, I drifted from one deck chair to another hoping the time would pass quickly. I heard a loud "toot!" of our steamship whistle and observed passenger excitement and waving on the starboard side of our ship as we passed the Hudson River Day Line steamship *Mary Powell* heading north.

The steamship *Mary Powell* of the Hudson River Day Line
near the Hudson River Palisades

The breeze was strong but warm when I found a seat near the stern of the ship to rest awhile. I closed my eyes and planned my trip home from the Desbrosses Street pier. I expected to be tired from my trip, but I was truly fatigued. It would be close to sunset when I reached my residence, and fortunately I planned a day to rest before resuming my profession.

I was awakened from my brief slumber by a steamship employee saying, "Yonkers," as he walked our deck, making sure no one missed their departure. I confirmed by my watch and schedule that we would arrive at Desbrosses Street pier in about ninety minutes. A short walk inside the main deck a newsstand I had observed earlier supplied me with a newspaper. The smell of cigars reminded me I had no more to smoke. Tempted to purchase one on board, I decided to wait and visit my favorite smoke shop on 5th Avenue when I returned to my normal schedule.

Steamships passing on the Hudson River

Finding a plush, comfortable chair in the lounge near the restaurant provided the opportunity to relax, read and peruse the news I missed. Although it was *The Tribune*, a New York City paper, a politician spouted on the front page about a trip to upstate New York.

"Visiting the farmers while they were getting in their crops, merchants in their stores, lawyers and doctors in their offices, and the manufacturers, mechanics and workmen in their factories, mills and workshops, I was assured that the Republicans I met were ready to deposit their votes for Benjamin Harrison and Whitelaw Reid."

As *The Tribune* was owned by Reid, his preference for using the newspaper for his own gain was quite apparent.

Also, I was confident no one in Liz's town or county was ever visited by this politician, and convinced he was unknown north of Yonkers. "What do these New York politicians understand about the needs of a Catskill farmer or sawmill owner?" I asked myself. Would Whitelaw Reid, if asked, be able to provide the price of a bushel of wheat?

Another newspaper article encouraged me to check the weather in front of our steamship. It read, "The four masted steam schooner, Walter Armington, arrived in Montauk, Rhode Island partly wrecked, having been struck by lightning at sea off Montauk Point Sunday night. The bolt struck the mizzenmast and splintered it, breaking the rigging. The mizzen topmast came down and smashed two of the three life boats, and the other was carried away."

Fortunately, the skies were mostly clear when we pulled into Yonkers.

Knowing that the west bank of the Hudson was now New Jersey meant we were close to New York City. The untarnished natural beauty of the Hudson shore continually diminished as we moved closer to the city. The repetition of industries such as brick kilns and shipping ports had now replaced the green and brown squares which defined the north country we left hours ago.

Spires of churches were visible above the clusters of buildings that were becoming more common as we pulled into the West 129th Street Pier. I moved to the port side as I watched the city move by and our ship passed numerous fishing and pleasure boats. When we pulled into the West 42nd Street Pier I began to smell the unique combination of urban industry, street vendor food and more that defined the aroma of the city I loved.

The crowded streets and buildings continued from one block to another in neat rows indistinguishable from one another. When we reached the Desbrosses Street Pier I stood on the lower deck near the ship's crew and watched as they dropped the gangplanks and secured the boat. I thanked the crew for their service, departed the ship and claimed my luggage.

Returned to familiar surroundings I quickly secured a ride on a Canal Street horse trolley to Broadway. Another horse trolley supplied my transportation to Houston and Broadway, and from there I walked to my apartment. Although my trip from the pier was quick and uneventful, never did I notice a tree or a blade of grass sway in the breeze as we moved swiftly through the city.

Everyone seemed in a hurry; no one appeared to take time to enjoy their surroundings. It was getting slightly darker as I reached my apartment building, and I turned to look for the sunset, but I could not see the sun anywhere through the congested buildings. I walked upstairs, unlocked my apartment, opened my luggage, and placed my new knife on the chest of drawers.

The air in the room was stale, and the street sounds seemed especially loud when I opened a window. I removed my clothes, lay down, and enjoyed finally resting my weary body in my own bed. The scent of the pine pillow I placed next to my head immediately brought me back to the hotel, the mountains and Liz. As I closed my eyes and inhaled the delicate tree fragrance, my final thought of the day was what Herr Strand had said about Liz and me, *"Menschliche Natur."* ("Human Nature."). I laughed quietly at the thought and fell asleep.

Author's Biography

Paul H. Zimmerman earned his Bachelor of Professional Studies at the State University of New York, Brockport. He has worked in the computer industry for over 40 years, first as a computer programmer, then as the president and owner of Computer Concepts, (http://www.ccforweb.com), a web design firm. Mr. Zimmerman is the author of three internationally published textbooks on web development, including one of the world's first college textbooks on Hypertext Markup Language (HTML), the language of the Internet. Now retired, he taught computer science at Aquinas College in Grand Rapids, Michigan for over twenty years. He enjoys competitive pistol and rifle shooting. He also enjoys playing the piano, composing, and recording his original music. You can listen to his music on your favorite digital media sources including Spotify, iTunes, and pandora.

Made in the USA
Columbia, SC
29 July 2024

f40a4b39-55e3-4f8c-add6-0af72a307b6fR01